I0531005

The Labyrinth of the World and the Paradise of the Heart

John Amos Comenius

Must Have Books
503 Deerfield Place
Victoria, BC
V9B 6G5
Canada

ISBN 9781773239606

Copyright 2022 – Must Have Books

CONTENTS

J. A. KOMENSKÝ

Every creature, even an irrational one, naturally inclines to delight in pleasure and comfort, and to desire them; so much the more man, by reason of his innate rational powers, aspires to the good and the comfortable. Indeed, his reason not only awakens the desire, but spurs him to seek and aspire to a thing more assiduously, the greater its proportion of the good, the pleasant, and the comfortable. Therefore, the question arose long ago among the wise wherein and what is the highest good (summum bonum) which could completely satisfy all human desires; that is, what could give a man such a complete satisfaction, that having obtained it, his mind could and must rest, for there would be nothing else he could desire.

Considering this matter carefully, we find that the problem has always been and is now engaging the attention not only of philosophers, who have been striving to solve it; but in addition, every man concerns himself with the problem where and how he may find complete happiness. We find, however, that almost all men seek it outside themselves, in the world and its possessions, imagining thus to pacify their minds: one in property and wealth, another in pleasure and indulgence, another in glory and honors, another in wisdom and learning, another among boon companions, and so forth. In short, all strive for things that are external, and seek in them their happiness.

But Solomon, the wisest of men, bears witness that satisfaction is not to be found in things, for after he had traveled through the world in search of rest for his own mind, he finally concluded: "I hated this life, because the work that is wrought under the sun is grievous unto me; for all is vanity, and vexation of spirit." When later he found true rest for his mind, he pronounced that it consisted in renouncing the world such as it is, and in having regard only for the Lord God, in fearing Him, and observing His commandments. For, he said, this is the whole duty of man. Similarly, David concluded that the happiest man is he who dismisses the world from his sight and mind, and cleaving to God alone, and having Him for his portion, dwells with Him in his heart.

May the mercy of God be praised that He opened my eyes also, so that I was able to perceive the manifold vanities of this pretentious world, as well as the frauds everywhere, hidden under the appearance of outward splendor. I have learned to seek peace and security of mind elsewhere. Desiring to portray this more vividly both to myself and to others, I have devised this peregrination or wandering through the world, recounting the perversities which I saw and encountered, and how I finally had discovered the desired solace, so vainly sought in the world. All this I have depicted in the present treatise. How wittily it was done, I do not care; may God grant that it be of benefit both to myself and to my fellow-men.

What you will read, dear reader, is no fable, even though it may have the appearance of one: it describes real life, as you will perceive when you have gained insight into it, particularly such among yu as are somewhat acquainted with my life and circumstances. For I have described, for the greatest part, the vicissitudes of the few years of my own life; for the rest, the incidents were observed in other lives, or I have been told f them. I have not, however, narrated all my experiences, partly from a sense of shame, and partly because I did not consider them of edification to others.

My guides, who are the guides of every man groping through the world, are indeed these two: insatiability of Mind, which pries into everything, and Custom, which lends a color of truth to all the frauds of the world. Nevertheless, if you apply your reason to them, you will perceive, as I did, the miserable confusion of our race; should it appear otherwise, you may feel sure that you are looking through the eye-glasses of general deception, which present all things to your view upside down.

As regards the portrayal of the happy life of the God-devoted hearts, that is professedly a sketch of their ideal state, rather than a description of the actual condition of all the elect. But the Lord has no lack even of such perfected spirits, and every truly devout person reading this book is in duty bound to desire the same degree of perfection. Fare you well, my dear Christian, and may the leader of light, the Holy Spirit, reveal to you,

better than I am able to do,

the vanity of the world, as well as the true glory, consolation,

and the joy of the elect and God-united hearts.

CHAPTER I

REASONS FOR UNDERTAKING THE WANDERINGS

Having reached the age when human intelligence begins to distinguish between good and evil, and having seen the various classes, orders, callings, occupations, and professions that men engage in, it seemed to me highly desirable to consider well which of these groups of folk I should join and which profession I should choose for my life work.

FICKLENESS OF MIND

2 After spending much time and thought on this problem, and having earnestly considered it, I finally decided to live with the least amount of trouble and labor with the greatest degree of comfort, peace, and good cheer.

3 However, I found it difficult to discover which profession this might be. Moreover, I did not know with whom to take proper counsel about the matter. For I was unwilling to ask the advice of just anyone, presuming that each would naturally praise his own calling. On the other hand, I was loath to undertake anything in a hurry for fear of erring.

4 Nevertheless, I confess that I secretly attempted to take up now one, then another or a third thing, but soon dropped them all again, perceiving (as I thought) difficulties and trivialities in all of them. Meantime, I feared that my fickleness might bring me into derision; accordingly, I knew not what to do.

5 After much inward struggle and hesitation, it finally occurred to me to investigate first all human affairs under the sun, and after I had intelligently compared them one with another, to choose the profession that would enable me to live pleasantly and peacefully. The longer I thought of this plan, the better I liked it.

  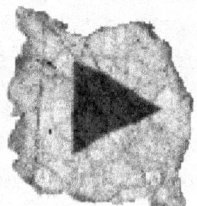

CHAPTER II

THE PILGRIM OBTAINS MR. UBIQUITOUS FOR HIS GUIDE

Thereupon I sauntered out by myself and began to consider where and how I should begin. Then suddenly, I know not whence, there appeared before me a brisk-gaited, spry-looking, and loquacious fellow whose feet, eyes, and tongue were as if on a turn-table. He approached me, inquiring where I had come from and whither I was going. I answered him that I had left my home to travel about the world in order to gain knowledge.

THE WORLD A LABYRINTH

2 He approved, but added: "But where is your guide?" "I have none; I trust God and my eyes not to lead me astray, " I answered. "You will accomplish nothing," he replied; "have you ever heard of the Cretan labyrinth?" "Yes, a little," I assented. "It was one of the wonders of the world," he continued; "a building with so many rooms, partitions, and passages that anyone entering it without a guide was doomed to wander and grope about it without ever finding his way out. That, however, was a mere joke in comparison with the arrangement of the labyrinth of this world, especially in our day. Take the advice of an experienced man and do not trust yourself into it alone!"

DESCRIPTION OF AN INSOLENT MAN

3 "But where shall I seek such a guide?" I inquired. "It is my work, " he answered, "to conduct those whose desire to see and investigate the world, and to guide and show them whatever there is; that is why I came to meet you." "Who are you, my dear fellow?" I asked in amazement. "My name is Searchall, and I am nicknamed Ubiquitous," he replied. "I go up and down the world peering into all its nooks and inquiring into what men say and do. I see all that is to be seen and ferret and spy out all that is secret. In short, nothing should be done without me, for it is my duty to oversee all things. If you follow me, I would let you into many secrets which you otherwise could never find alone."

4 Hearing such news, I was overjoyed to find such a leader and begged him not to consider it troublesome to guide me through the world. "Gladly I serve others," he replied, "gladly shall I serve you." Thereupon, taking me by the hand, he said: "Let us go!" So we started, I remarking: "I am indeed curious to see the course of the world, and whether one can safely rely on anything." Hearing this, my companion stopped and said: "My friend, if you are undertaking this journey, intending to judge what you see in accordance with your own opinions instead of being pleased with whatever you find, I know not how Her Majesty, our Queen, will be satisfied."

VANITY, THE QUEEN OF THE WORLD

5 "And who is your Queen?" I inquired. "She who directs the world and its entire course from one end to the other," he replied. "Her name is Wisdom, although some dunces dub her Vanity. Let me warn you beforehand against prying overmuch into things, when we journey about and investigate, or you will come to grief, and so may I!"

  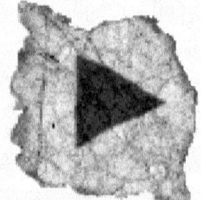

CHAPTER III

MR. DELUSION JOINS THE TRAVELLERS

while he was thus conversing with me, someone appeared at our side--I could not tell whether it was a man or a woman (for the fellow was strangely disguised and as if in a haze). "Where are you taking this man, Ubiquitous?" he inquired. "On a world tour," replied my companion; "for he desires to examine it."

2 "Why without me?" queried the stranger, "you know that it is your duty to guide, while it is mine to show whatever there is to see. It is Her Majesty's will that no one, having entered her realm, should himself interpret, as he pleases, what he sees and hears, indulging his own wit. For the scenes should be explained to him and he remain content therewith."

3 "Is there anyone so insolent as not to accept our order, just as all the rest do?" retorted Ubiquitous, "nevertheless, it seems to me that this fellow may require a bridle. Come along, then!" The stranger joined us, and we continued our journey.

HABITS OF DELUDING THE WORLD

4 I, however, thought to myself: "I hope to God that I shall not be misled. These fellows intend to place some sort of bridle on me." Thereupon, I spoke to the newcomer: "Friend, do not be offended; but I would like to know your name." "I am the interpreter of Wisdom, Queen of the world, and am under her orders to instruct men how all things in the world ought to be understood," he answered. "Accordingly, I instill into the minds of all you will meet, both old and young, well-born and commoners, foolish and learned, all that pertains to true worldly wisdom. Thus I give them joy and contentment. For without me even kings, princes, nobles, and all the most distinguished people would find themselves in a strange state of despondency, and would pass their earthly days in sorrow."

5 "How fortunate that God has sent you as my guide, dear friend, if what you say is true!" I exclaimed, "for I have started on this journey in order to find the most reliable and delightful thing in the world, so that I may lay hold of it. Having you for my counsellor, I shall be able to choose more easily." "Have no doubt about it," he rejoined, "for although you will find everything in our kingdom excellently and splendidly ordered and jolly, and will learn that all who are willing to obey our Queen never fail of a comfortable living; it is, nevertheless, true that some professions or businesses have more comfort and leisure than others. You will be able to choose among them as you please. I shall explain all that is necessary to you." "What then is your name?" I inquired. "My name is Delusion."

  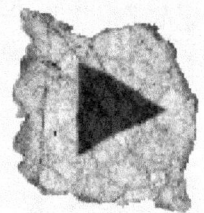

CHAPTER IV

THE PILGRIM IS BRIDLED AND BESPECTACLED

Hearing this, I was horrified at the thought of what fine companions I had acquired. One of them (I mused) had made mention of a bridle. The other was named Delusion. He spoke of his Queen as Vanity (although that seemed to have been an unguarded slip of the tongue). What next?

2 Accordingly, as I walked on in silence, with downcast eyes and unwilling, halting steps, Searchall exclaimed: "How now, you weathercock, I suspect you are minded to turn back!" Before I had time to answer, he threw a bridle over my neck, the bit of which slipped quickly into my mouth. He remarked at the same time: "Now you will be more willing to persevere in what you have begun."

THE BRIDLE OF VANITY

3 I examined the bridle and found it was made of the headstall of Curiosity, the bit having been forged of the steel of Tenacity in undertakings. Then I understood that I should no longer journey through the world of my own will, as I had intended, but should be forcibly driven on by my mind's curiosity and my insatiable thirst for knowledge.

4 Just then Delusion on the other side remarked: "For my part, I present you with these glasses through which you must examine the world." After he fixed the glasses on my nose, everything immediately assumed a changed aspect. For they had the power (as I have tested many times afterwards) of making distant objecdts appear near and the near distant, of the small large and the large small, of the ugly things beautiful and the beautiful ugly, of the black white and the white black, and so on. Hence, I realized that it was not without good reason that he was called Delusion, since he could not make and impose such glasses upon mankind.

GROUND FROM ASSUMPTION AND HABIT

5 As I learned later, the lenses were ground from the glass of Assumption, and were set in horn-rims called Habit.

6 Fortunately, he placed them askew on my nose, so that they did not fit me properly and did not prevent me, when I raised my head, from looking under them and thus seeing things in their proper, natural aspect. This gladdened me, and I thought to myself: even though you stop my mouth and cover my eyes, yet I trust God that you will not be able to restrain my reason and my mind. I will go and see what kind of world this is that my Lady Vanity desires us to examine in her own fashion, but forbids us to look at with our own eyes!

CHAPTER V

THE PILGRIM LOOKS UPON THE WORLD FROM ABOVE

BEYOND THE WORLD THERE IS NOTHING. While I was thus musing, we suddenly found ourselves (I know not how) upon an exceedingly high tower, so that I seemed to touch the clouds. Looking down from this tower, I saw a city beautiful in appearance, shining, and prodigiously wide-spread, but not so great that I could not discern its limits and boundaries all around. The city formed a circle, and was surrounded with walls and ramparts, but instead of moats there yawned a gloomy abyss, to all appearances boundless and bottomless. Light shone only above the city, while beyond the walls it was pitch dark.

2 THE SITUATION OF THE WORLD. The city itself, as I perceived, was divided into innumerable streets, squares, houses and buildings both large and small. It swarmed with people as if with insects. Toward the east I saw a gate, from which an alley ran toward another gate facing the west. The second gate opened upon the streets of the city. I counted six principal streets running from east to west, parallel with each other. In the midst of these streets was a very large ring or marketplace. Farthest toward the west, upon a steep and rocky eminence, stood a lofty, magnificent castle toward which the inhabitants of the city frequently gazed.

3 THE GATE OF ENTERING AND THE GATE OF SEPARATION. My guide, Mr. Ubiquitous, remarked: "Behold, my pilgrim, here you have that fine world that you were so anxious to see! I brought you first to this elevation that you might survey it all and thus might understand its arrangement. The eastern gate is the gate of life, through which all who dwell on earth must enter. That other gate which is nearer to us is the gate of division, where all receive their lot in life and turn toward one or another calling.

4 SIX CLASSES OF THE WORLD. "The streets which you see are the various classes, orders, and professions in which men are settled. Observe the six principal streets: in the one toward the south dwells the domestic group--parents, children and servants; in the next dwell the craftsmen and the tradesman; in the third, nearest the market-place, are found the learned professions, devoted to the intellectual labors; on the other side, opposite them, is the clerical order, to which the rest resort for religious ministrations; beyond them are the governing and magisterial classes; and farthest to the north is the order of knights engaged in military affairs. How excellent it all is! The first beget all; the second sustain all; the third teach all; the fourth pray for all; the fifth judge and preserve good order among all; and the sixth fight for all. Thus all serve one another, and all live in harmony with each other.

5 THE CASTLE OF FORTUNE. "The castle toward the west is Arx Fortunate , the Castle of Fortune , where only the most distinguished people dwell in the enjoyment of wealth, pleasure, and glory.

THE COMMON SQUARE AND THE CASTLE OF THE WORLD. The central square is common to all. There men of all classes come together to transact their necessary business. In the center of it, as the hub of everything else, stands the residence of Wisdom, the queen of the world."

6 THE BEGINNING OF CONFUSION. I was pleased with this excellent arrangement and began to praise God for having disposed all classes in such splendid order. But one thing I disliked, namely, that streets intersected each other in many places, so that here and there they ran together. It seemed that this might result in confusion and straying. Moreover, as I gazed at the global shape of the world, I palpably felt it move and whirl in a circle until I feared to be overcome with dizziness. For wherever I cast my glance, everything to the least mote seemd to swarm before my eyes. Moreover, when I stopped to listen, the air was filled with the sounds of pounding, striking, shuffling, whispering, and screaming.

7 THERE WAS DELUSION TOO. My interpreter, Mr. Delusion, remarked: "You see, my dear fellow, how delightful this world is, and how splendid are all things in it, even though you view it only from afar. What will you say when you examine it in detail and with all its delights? Who would not be happy to live in such a world?" "I am much pleased with it from a distance, " I answered: "how it shall be later on, I cannot tell." "All will be well, believe me, " he replied: "but now let us go."

8 THE WAYS OF CHILDHOOD. "Wait, " Mr. Ubiquitous interposed, "let me show him from here what otherwise we do not intend to visit. Turn back toward the east: do you discern something crawling out of the dark gate and creeping toward us?" "Yes, I see it, " I replied. "Those are human beings, " he continued, "just entering the world. They themselves know not whence

(for as yet they are not self-conscious) nor do they know themselves to be human. Hence, darkness envelopes them, and they merely wail and cry. But as they proceed up the street, the darkness slowly disappears and the light increases, until they reach the gate beneath us. Let us now go and see what transpires there."

CHAPTER VI

FATE DISTRIBUTES CALLINGS

GATE, THE SENTINEL OF THE WORLD. We descended a dark, winding staircase and entered the gate in which a large hall was filled with young people. On the right sat a fierce-looking old man holding a large copper pot in his hand. I noticed that all who arrived from the Gate of Life presented themselves before him and each, putting his hand into the pot, drew out a piece of paper inscribed with a word. Thereupon, he went toward one of the streets, either running and joyfully shouting, or walking with a sorrowful mien, complaints, grimaces, and backward glances.

2 DISTRIBUTING OF OCCUPATIONS. I approached nearer and took a look at some of the slips. One read, Rule! ; another, Serve! ; or Command! ; or Obey! ; or Write! ; or Study! ; or Hoe! ; or Judge! ; or Fight! ; and so on. I was amazed at the scene. Mr. Searchall explained it by saying: "Here are distributed the callings and occupations in accordance with which each person is allotted his lifework. He who directs these lots is called Fate , and all who enter the world must receive his assignment."

3 THE PILGRIM WANTS FIRST TO EXAMINE ALL. Just then Mr. Delusion nudged me, indicating that I, too, should draw a lot. But I begged that I might not be assigned to any particular occupation (until I had first examined it) in order not to entrust my lot, come what may, to blind chance. I was told, however, that without the knowledge and consent of the lord regent, Fate, such an exception was not permitted. Stepping up to him, therefore, I humbly presented my petition: that I came with the intention of examining all things before I would make my choice of what would most appeal to me.

4 AND HE OBTAINED PERMISSION. "Son, " he answered, "you see that others do not do so, but abide by what they receive or what happens to fall to them. But since you desire it so much, I consent. " Having then inscribed on a slip of paper the word Speculare! (i.e., Examine or Investigate), he handed it to me, thus dismissing me.

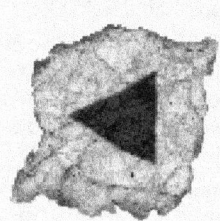  

CHAPTER VII

THE PILGRIM EXAMINES THE MARKET PLACE OF THE WORLD

HE SEES THE DIVERSITY OF MEN. Thereupon, my guide remarked: "Since you wish to investigate all things, let us begin by visiting the market place." He immediately led me there. And behold! such countless multitudes were gathered there that they seemed like a mist. People of all nations and languages of the world, of every age, stature, class, order, and profession, as well as both sexes, were gathered there. As I gazed at them, they were milling about hither and thither like bees at swarming time, or even more strangely.

2 THEIR CHARACTERS AND GESTURES. For some were wandering about, others were running or driving, or stood still, while another group was sitting or lying down. One group was rising while anothing was lying down, or was squirming about. Some were alone, others in large or small companies. Their costume and appearance also differed most widely: some indeed were stark naked, gesticulating queerly. When some of them met, they gestured with their hands, mouths, knees and otherwise, or huddled and cuddled....they cut all kinds of capers. "Here you see the noble human kind, those delightful, reasonable, and immortal creatures, bearing the image and likeness of immortal God, as may be learned from the great variety of their glorious deeds, " my companion declaimed: "here you may behold as in a mirror the dignity of your kind."

3 HYPOCRISY IN ALL OF THEM. I examined them more keenly, therefore, and observed, in the first place, that each one of those milling in the crowd wore a mask on his face, but when he was alone or with his equals, he took it off. However, as soon as he rejoined the crowd, he put it on again. I inquired what this meant. My guide answered: "That, my dear son, is human prudence, so as not to appear to everyone as one really is. Alone, one needs not constrain himself: but among people it befits one to appear decorously and to give a seemly appearance to one's affairs." I was seized by a desire to examine more diligently how these people appeared without artificial make-up.

4 THEIR DIVERSE DEFORMITIES. And watching them attentively, I saw that they were all variously disfigured, not merely in their features, but in their bodies as well. Most of them were pimply, scabby, or leprous. Besides, one had a swine lip, another dog's teeth, or ox horns, or ass ears, or basilisk eyes, or a fox tail, or wolf claws. Some, I observed, strutted about with a proudly erected peacock's neck, others with an erect lapwing crest, or with horse-hoofs, and so on. Most of them resembled monkeys. Horrified, I exclaimed: "But I see monsters here!" "Of what monsters are you babbling, you meddler?" remarked my interpreter, threatening me with his fist; "if only you look properly through your glasses, you will recognize them as human!" Moreover, some of the passers-by overheard my calling them monsters and stopped, threatening and reviling me. I realized that it was useless to argue. Therefore I remained silent, thinking to myself: if they wish to regard themselves as human, so be it. But I see what I see. Moreover, I was afraid lest my companion should readjust the glasses and thus delude. I decided, therefore, to be quiet and rather to concentrate on those fine things of which I had seen the beginning. I looked about me again and noticed that many people were dexterous in the manipulation of their masks, quickly snatching them off and donning them again, so that in an instant they could assume any appearance which befitted their need. Then I began to understand the course of the world. Nevertheless, I held my peace.

5 THEIR MUTUAL UNDERSTANDINGS. I also observed and heard that they spoke to each other in different languages. Consequently, for the greatest part they did not understand each other, and either did not answer or replied each one differently. In some places a large crowd gathered, all speaking at the same and each holding forth, none listening to the rest, although they tried to secure a hearing for themselves by pulling others toward them. Nevertheless, even so they failed, often bringing on fights and scuffles. "In God's name, is this the Tower of Babel?" I exclaimed: "everybody plays his own fiddle, could there be any greater confusion?"

6 PREOCCUPATION WITH USELESS MATTERS. There were among them but few idlers, for the majority occupied themselves with some work or other. Yet their occupations (and I should have never suspected) were but childish games, or at most drudgery. For some of them were gathering rubbish and distributing it among themselves; others were rolling timber and stones back and forth, or hoisting them on pulleys and lowering them again; others were digging in the ground, or conveying or carrying soil from place to place; the rest were working with bells, mirrors, bellows, rattles, and other trinkets. Some were even playing with their own shadow, measuring, chasing, or grasping at it. All this was done so assiduously that many sighed and perspired, while others fainted with fatigue. Moreover, there were officers stationed everywhere who directed and allotted the tasks with great zeal, while the workers obeyed with equal alacrity. Filled with astonishment, I exclaimed: "Alas! was then man made for wasting the keenness of his divinely-given talents upon such vain and petty toil?" "What is vain about it?" retorted my interpreter; "does it not appear as in a mirror how all problems are solved by human

ingenuity? One engages in one thing, another in something else." "But all, " I said, "are busied with useless drudgery which is unworthy of their glorious eminence." "Do not play the wiseacre," he replied; "they are not in heaven yet, but are still on earth and must deal with earthly things. Observe, by the way, in what an orderly fashion everything is done."

7 TERRIBLE DISORDER. Again examining them, I noticed that nothing more disorderly could be invented. For while someone was staggering and stumbling under a load, another came and meddled with him; this led to brawls, fights, and scuffles. Then they became reconciled, only to tear each other soon afterwards. Sometimes several caught hold of the same thing; then they all dropped it and ran away, each in a different direction. Those who were subject to officers and overseers did what they were told willy-nilly, because they had to; but even there I saw much confusion. Some broke ranks and fled, while others grumbled at their foremen, refusing to do what they had ordered. Some snatched the overseers' cudgels from them and robbed them. Hence, all was in a hubbub. But since they were wont to call it orderly, I dared not say them nay.

CHAPTER VIII

THE PILGRIM OBSERVES THE MARRIED ESTATE AND ITS ORDER

THE PREPARATION FOR IT IS TOILSOME AND WISTFUL. My companions then led me to a street where, they said, the married people lived, as a good demonstration of the mode of that delightful life. And behold! there stood a gate which, according to the guide, was called Engagement. Before it was spread a spacious square full of both sexes who were walking about and peering into each other's eyes and examining each other's ears, nose, teeth, tongue, hands, feet, and other limbs. They likewise measured how tall, broad, stout or slender each was. They approached or receded from one another, examining each other carefully now from the front, then the back, the left, the right side, testing all they saw. Especially were they curious (as I have seen most frequently) about each other's purses, money-bags, and pocketbooks, measuring and weighing how long and wide, full, tight, or thin they were. Occasionally several men pointed at the same woman, at other times none. If any man tried to drive the others away, they quarreled, exchanged blows, and fought with each other; sometimes even murders occurred, as I observed. At times one drove away his rival, only to be himself chased away in turn; another, routing a group of rivals, himself thereupon ran away also. Some lost no time in examining, but seized the nearest he could grasp. Thereupon, the couple led each other hand in hand toward the gate. Seeing such trivialities all about me, I inquired what those people were doing. "They would like to settle in the Street of Matrimony, " my interpreter answered, "but since choosing a mate most suitable to himself. Whoever has found his mate goes, as you see, with his spouse, to the gate." "The process seems unusually laborious, " I remarked; "can it not be facilitated somehow?" "This is no labor, " he answered, "but sheer delight. Do you not see how jolly they are about it, how they laugh, sing, and shout? Believe me, there is no more joyful life than this." I looked and observed that some indeed were laughing and shouting: but others went about with downcast mien and woebegone expression, restless and moping, plunging hither and yon, despondent, sleepless, without appetite, and even delirious. "How about these?" I inquired. "Even that is a delight," my interpreter answered. "So be it then, " I replied; "let us go and see what happens thereafter."

2 GREAT UNCERTAINTY ABOUT THE OUTCOME. Forcing our way through the crowds, we came to the gate itself, but before we entered, I noticed a pair of scales there, consisting of two baskets, and crowds of people stood about them. A man and a woman were placed opposite each other into the baskets on the scales. Only after the couples had spent much time weighing were they permitted to proceed through the gate. But not all fared equally well. For some fell through the basket, and amid much laughter, were obliged to pick themselves up and with shame to clear off. Besides, they had a hood or a sack thrust over their ears, and were made the butt of the crowd. Observing this, I inquired: "What is going on here?" My companion answered: "This is their engagement, when all conditions appear favorable. If the scales indicate equality and all seems favorable, they are admitted to the marriage state, as you see; but if there is an inequality, they separate." "What equality is to be seen here?" I exclaimed; "for I plainly perceive that some are, according to the scales, equal in age, class and otherwise, yet they cause one of them to fall through the basket; others are, on the contrary, extremely unequal, as when a dotard is mated with a lassie, or a lad with an old hag, one stands up straight, the other is bent double, yet they say that all is well. How can that be?" "You do not see all," he answered; "it is true that some of these grey-beards and grandames would not, by themselves, weigh a pound of peasecods; but when they possess a fat pocket-book, or a hat before which other hats are +6doffed, or something else of the kind (for such things always have their weight) it happens that matters do not...

INDISSOLUBILITY REGARDLESS OF THE OUTCOME. Following those who entered the gate, I then saw between the gates several blacksmiths fettering each couple into frightful handcuffs; only when thus bound together were they allowed to proceed further. Many people, invited for the purpose, were present as witnesses (as I was told) of the fettering ceremony. They played and sang for the couples and told them to be of good cheer. Observing carefully, I perceived that the cuffs were not padlocked as is ordinarily done with prisoners, but were forged, welded and soldered together to prevent the couple from ever unlocking or breaking them during their lifetimes. At this I was frightened and exclaimed: "Oh, can there be a more horrible prison than this, from which there is never a hope of deliverance?" "It is true that of all human bonds this is the strongest, " answered my interpreter; "but there is no reason to fear it. For the sweetness of this estate causes the yoke to be gladly assumed. You will see for yourself what a pleasant life it is." "Let us go among them, then, that I may see," I urged.

LITTLE PLEASURE EVEN MARRIAGE IS MOST SUCCESSFUL. Thereupon we entered the street and saw a great multitude of these people, always in pairs. However, many of them seemed to me to have been very unequally yoked, large with small, handsome with ugly, young with old, and so on. Watching them closely in order to find what they were doing and what the sweetness of that state consisted of, I observed that they gazed at each other, conversed together, and occasionally even caressed or kissed one another. "Here you see what a fine thing a successful marriage is, " remarked my interpreter. "Is this then the whole sum of it at its very best?" I asked. "Of course!" he answered. "That certainly is little enough; and whether or not it is worth the fetters, I know not."

5 MISERY AND DRUDGERY OF ALL MARRIED PEOPLE GENERALLY. Thereupon, I resumed my observation and perceived with how much toil and anxiety the poor wretches were burdened. The majority had a row of children harnessed to themselves. The children were screaming and squalling, stenching and fouling, sickening and dying, not to mention the pain, tears, and the risk of life with which they had been brought into the world. If any of them grew up, this imposed a twofold task: to hold him bridled, and to spur him on to follow his parents' footsteps. For sometimes they suffered neither the bridle nor the spur but caused their parents much trouble, weariness, and tears. When the parents gave them free rein, or the children tore themselves away, the result was shame and even death for the parents. Observing these things here and there, I began to exhort both parents and children: the former against mawkish love and excessive indulgence of their children; the latter to certain virtues. I gained but little thereby, except to earn dark looks and caustic remarks, and even to be threatened with death. Thereupon, I praised the childless, some of whom I noticed there; but they lamented and complained that they were without consolation. Thus I understood that in the married life both to have and not to have children is misery. Besides, almost every couple had servants attached to themselves and to the household for waiting upon them and their families, whose comfort the pair were obliged to consider before their own or that of their family, often at a considerable trouble to themselves. Above all, there was strewn about, just as in the market place, a great deal of baggage, timber, obstacles, boulders, and pits; when any stumbled and injured himself, his mate was obliged to endure his whimpering, weeping, and pain, not being able to get away. Accordingly, I learned that in married life instead of one care, anxiety, or danger each must bear as many cares, anxieties, and dangers as he had yoke-fellows. Consequently I conceived a dislike for this life.

6 THE AWFUL TRAGEDY OF AN UNSUCCESSFUL MARRIAGE. Besides, I observed some tragic cases in this group. For not a few among those yoked together were of contrary temperaments, one wished one thing, the other the opposite; one desiring to go one way, the other another; thereupon they quarreled, scolded, and bit each other. One complained to the passers-by of one thing, the other of another. When there was no one to arbitrate between them, they fell upon each other, lay about with fists, beat and belabored one another horribly. If someone succeeded in pacifying them, in a short time they were at each other's throats again. Sometimes, after a long quarrel, whether to go right or left, both persisting obstinately in their respective decisions, they finally threw themselves with all their might in opposite directions; here was a tug of war and a spectacle as to who would pull the other over! Sometimes the man won, and the wife, in spite of her efforts to hold on to soil, grass, or anything else she could grasp, was dragged over to his side. At other times the man was dragged after his wife, which caused much jeering among the spectators. However, it seemed to me a matter worthier of pity than of laughter. Especially when I saw how in their misery they wept, sighed, and stretched their hands toward heaven, offering gold and silver if only they might be delivered from their bondage. I asked the interpreter: "Is there any possibility of helping them? May not these people who cannot agree with each be freed and permitted to separate?" "It cannot be," he answered, "they must remain together as long as they live." "Oh, is there anything more cruel than this slavery? It is worse than death itself!" I exclaimed. "Why did not they think it through before?" he retorted; "it serves them right!"

VOLUNTARY SLAVERY. Just then I observed Death with her arrows piercing and felling some of them; whereupon their fetters instantly burst asunder. I was glad for their sake, imagining that they themselves had wished it and would be sincerely glad of their deliverance. But behold, almost every one of them burst into tears and wailing such as I had scarcely heard before in the world; they wrung their hands and lamented their misfortune. I could understand that those whom I had previously seen living together in peace really felt bereaved. I presumed, however, that the othersd were merely pretending before men, although in reality they would know how to repent, and I was ready to wager that they would advise others to avoid the fetters. On the contrary, before I had time to realize, and almost before they had dried their tears, they hurried outside the gate and came back in bonds. "Oh, you miserable wretches, you are not worthy to be pitied!" I cried angrily. Then turning to my guide, I said: "Let us go away; I see more deceit than anything else in this estate."

CHAPTER IX

THE PILGRIM EXAMINES THE LABOURING CLASS

WHAT HE SAW THERE GENERALLY. Proceeding, we entered the street inhabited by craftsmen, which was subdivided into many narrow alleys and smaller squares, and all about us we observed various halls, workshops, forges, benches, stores, and booths full of quaint-looking implements. Men plied these tools in a curious manner, with clattering, striking, squeaking, squealing, whistling, piping, blowing, blasting, jingling, and rattling. I saw some digging in the earth, either tearing up the surface of digging underneath like moles. Others were wading in water, rivers, or the sea; yet others were tending fires, gaping into the air, fighting wild beasts, dressing wood or stone, or carrying and hauling various commodities from place to place. My interpreter said to me: "Behold these brisk and cheerful occupations! Which of them do you like the best?" "There is doubtless some cheerfulness here, " I answered; "nevertheless, I also observe much drudgery and hear many groans along with it." "Not all work is so arduous, " he answered; "let us look closer and examine some these trades." So they led me through them one after another, and I scrutinized them all and tried my hand at one or another to test them; but to describe them all I am neither able nor willing. I shall not, however, keep secret what I concluded in general.

PERILOUS HASTE IN EVERY BUSINESS. In the first place, I saw that all these human ocupations were but toil and drudgery, and each had some disadvantages and dangers of its own. I saw that those who were working with fire were scorched and blackened like Moors: the clatter of hammers was ever jangling in their ears and had rendered them half-deaf; the glare of the fire had blinded their eyes; and their skin was perpetually singed. Those who were working underground had darkness and terrors for companions, and, as happened not infrequently, were liable to be buried alive. Those working in water were constantly soaked like roof-thatch, were shivering with cold like an aspen leaf, suffered from sclerosis of the viscera, and not a few of them fell a prey to the deep. Those who were working in wood, stone, and other heavy substances, were full of callouses, sighing, and exhaustion. Indeed, I saw some engaged in such asinine drudgery that they struggled and toiled to perspiration, exhaustion, collapse, injury, and finally to total breakdown; but despite all their miserable toil, they were hardly able to earn bread for themselves. Indeed, I observed others whose livelihoods were easier and more renumerative; but the less drudgery, the more vice and fraud there were.

ENDLESS HASTE. Secondly, I observed that men toiled only to feed their mouths; for whatever they earned, they crammed it all down their throats or the throats of their families, save in the rare cases when they stinted their mouths in order to put it into their bags. But, as I perceived, their bags were either torn, so that what they had put into them fell out again and others picked it up; or another came and snatched it out of their hands; or he himself, having tripped, dropped the bag or tore, or otherwise lost it. Thus I plainly saw that these human toils resembled water being poured from one glass into another; money was earned to be spent again, with the only difference that it was easier spent than earned, no matter whether it was crammed down the throat or hoarded in money coffers. Consequently, I sw everywhere many more poor than rich.

3 TOILSOME HASTE. Thirdly, I saw that every occupation required the whole man. If anyone but looked back or acted a little slowly, he was soon left behind and everything dropped from his hands. Hence, before he realized it, he found himself on the rocks.

DIFFICULT HASTE. In the fourth place, I observed many obstacles in the way. Before some one was started in business, a good portion of his life was gone; and after he was started, it did not look closely to his affairs, everything went against him; moreover, I noticed that even the most diligent among them met with loss as often as with profit.

HASTE PROVOKING ENVY. In the fifth place, I saw everywhere (especially among those engaged in the same kind of business) much envy and ill-will. If work piled up for one of them, or he enjoyed brisker trade than another, his neighbors gave him sour looks or gnashed their teeth at him, and whenever they could, wrecked his business: hence quarrels, disaffection, and cursing; some out of sheer despair threw away their tools and lapsed into idleness and voluntary poverty.

SINFUL HASTE. In the sixth place, I noticed everywhere much falsehood and fraud. Whatever anyone did, especially for a customer, was done shoddily and carelessly; yet he extolled and praised his own work to high heaven.

VAIN AND SUPERFLUOUS HASTE. In the seventh place, I found here a great deal of superfluity; and became firmly convinced that most of the occupations were but crass futility and useless folly. For the human body requires but frugal and plain food and drink, need be clothed with but plain and unostentatious garments; and be sheltered in a modest and simple house; but little and easily discharged care and labor are required, as was customary in ancient times. But I found that the world either could not or would not comprehend this simple truth, for now it is customary that stuffing and filling of the belly requires so many and such rare delicacies that the greater part of mankind is employed in their gathering on land and sea, and in this drudgery men waste their strength and hazard their lives; moreover, for the preparation of this food specially-trained masters must now be employed. Similarly, not a small part of humankind is engaged in building shelters and procuring materials for clothing and in tailoring them in various preposterous styles; all this is useless, superfluous, often even sinful. Likewise, I saw craftsmen whose entire art and occupation consisted of making childish trifles and other playthings, intended merely for amusement and the wasting of time. Others there were whose task was manufacturing and multiplyinge instruments of cruelty, such as swords, daggers, battle-maces, muskets, and so forth, all for the killing of men. How people can conscientiously and with a cheerful mind ply such trades I know not. But I know that if the useless, superfluous, and the sinful were excluded and eliminated from these trades, the greater part of the business of mankind would collapse. For this, as well as for the above-mentioned reasons, my mind could find no pleasure in any of them.

8 HASTE IS FOR BRUTES NOT MEN. My conclusion was strengthened when I saw that all these occupations were only of the body and for the body; while man, possessing a greater thing than the body--namely a soul--ought rather to bestow his principal care upon that and seek its well-being above all other +8things.

9 I wish to relate particularly how I fared among waggoners on land and sailors on the sea. For while I was examining the workshops and appeared discontented, Mr. Ubiquitous said to Mr. Delusion: "I notice that this fellow is or a roving disposition, a bit of quick silver, constantly desiring to be in motion: for he fancies nothing stable, not being willing to be tied to any one place. Let us show him a freer life: that of commerce in which he can roam at will from place to place and fly about like a bird." "I am not opposed to trying even that," I said. So we went.

HASTE OF A WAGGONER'S LIFE. Then I perceived a crowd of men rushing hither and thither, seeking and gathering all kinds of things such as splinters, soil, and manure, and hoisting and heaping them into loads. I inquired what they were doing. They replied: "They are getting ready to travel over the world." "But why not without the heavy load?" I asked; "they could drive more easily." "What a simpleton you are!" they retorted; "how could they drive? That is their wings." "Wings?" said I, "Of course, their wings! They provide resolution and incentive, and serve as passport and safe-conduct everywhere. Do you think that everybody is free to roam about the world at will? These people must secure their living, favor, and everything else from their occupation." So I looked; and behold they piled up as large a load as they could find, then slid and rolled it upon a kind of dolly on wheels, and tying it to the dolly, hitched some beasts to it and dragged the whole contraption laboriously and with great difficulty over hills, mountains, dales, and gullies, rejoicing in what they considered their excellent and cheerful life. At first it so appeared to me also. But when I observed how they occasionally got stuck in the mud and wallowed and waddled in it, pushing and pulling their loads, and perceived how much they endured from being exposed to rain, snow-storms, sleet, blizzards, frosts, and heat; and how they were waylaid at passes and robbed of their goods and purses (for on such occasions neither anger, swearing, nor threats were of any effect); finally when I saw how they were attacked on the roads by robber bands and how their very life was gravely jeopardized, I became disgusted with their occupation.

11 DISCOMFORT OF A SAILOR'S LIFE. Then my guides told me that they were was a more comfortable mode of travelling about the world, namely that of navigation; afloat, a man was not shaken so much, was not bespattered with mud, did not get stuck in a rut; moreover, he was shot from one end of the world to the other, everywhere finding something new, something he had not seen or heard of before. And they led me to the ends of the earth where nothing but sky and water stretched before us.

CHAPTER X

THE PILGRIM EXAMINES THE LEARNED CLASS GENERALLY

Thereupon my guide said to me: "At last I understand where your mind draws you: among the learned with you, among the learned; that is the bait for you, an easier, more peaceful, and for the mind a more useful life." "That is indeed so," said my interpreter; "for what can be more delightful for a man than to withdraw from, and to ignore unprofitable manual toil and give himself wholly to the investigation of all splendid causes? That is indeed what makes mortal men like, if not equal to, immortal God, so they may become as though omniscient, knowing and understanding what is, has been, or is to be in the heavens above, upon the earth, and in the abyss beneath; true, such perfection is not attained by all to an equal degree." "Lead me there, why do you tarry?" said I.

A RIGOROUS EXAMINATION TO START WITH. We then came to a gate called Discipline : it was long, narrow, and dark, full of armed guards, to whom every one desiring to enter the street of the learned had to report and request his guidance. I observed that the crowds of those who presented themselves, for the greates part young men, were immediately put through various severe examinations. The first of these, required of all, aimed at ascertaining what kind of purse, posterior, head, brain (which they judged by the nasal +11mucus), and skin each of the candidates brought. If the head were of steel, the brain of quicksilver, the posterior of lead, the skin of iron, and the purse of gold, they praised him and willingly conducted him farther; if he lacked any of these five prerequisites, they either ordered him back or admitted him grudgingly, foreboding ill success for him. I was amazed and inquired: "Does so much depend upon these five metals that they search for them so diligently?" "Very much, indeed," replied my interpreter; "the head that not of steel would crack: without the brain of quicksilver the pupil could not make a mirror of it; without the skin of sheet-iron he would not survive the formative process; not possessing the seat of lead, he would hatch nothing but miscarry everything; and without the purse of gold, where would he obtain the necessary leisure or teachers, both living and dead? Or do you imagine thatsuch great things may be obtained without cost?" Then only did I understand that this profession requires health, intelligence, perseverance, patience, and expenditure of money. "It may therefore be truly affirmed," I said, "non cuivis contingit adire +12Corinthum. Not every log is fit to serve for grained veneer."

TO ENTER IS PAINFUL AND DIFFICULT: MEMORIAL ARTIFICIALIS. We proceeded further into the gate where I observed that each guard, choosing one or more of the candidates, led them on, blew something into their ears, wiped their eyes, steamed their nose and nostrils, drew out and trimmed their tongue, taught them to clasp or extend their hands and fingers, and coached them in I do not know how many more ways. Some guards even attempted to bore their pupils' heads and to pour something into them. My interpreter, seeing frightened thereat, said "Be not amazed; the learned must possess hands, tongue, eyes, ears, brain, and all other external and internal organs of a different order from those of the ignorant masses of manking; for that purpose they are here reformed, and that cannot be accomplished without toil and pain." Then I looked and saw how deadly those poor wreteches had to pay for their re-formation. I do not speak of their purses, but of their skins which they had to expose. For they were beaten with fists, +13pointers, canes, and sticks on their cheeks, head, back, and seat until they shed blood, and were full of bruises and scars, weals and callouses. Some seeing this, before they surrendered themselves to the guards, cast but a hasty glance inside the gate and ran away: others tore themselves out of the hands of the would-be re-formers and likewise fled. Only a small remnant persevered to the end, to proceed further into the square; desirous of joining that profession, I too underwent the formation in a like manner, although not without hardships and +14bitterness.

EACH LEARNED MAN IS GIVEN A PASSWORD. When we left the gate, I noticed that each of those who had acquired something of the preliminary training, received a device by which he could be recognized as belonging to the scholars: an ink-horn stuck under his belt, a pen behind his ear, and a blank book for recording knowledge in his hand; I too received those articles. Mr. Searchall thereupon said to me: "We are now confronted with four paths: philosophy, medicine, law, and theology; where shall we go first?" "Do as you judge best," I replied. "Let us first go to the square where they all meet, " he suggested; "you will there see them all together, then let us visit their lecture rooms separately."

5 EVEN AMONG LEARNED MEN THERE ARE DEFICIENCIES. Thereupon, he led me to a square and behold! a crowd of students, masters, doctors, priests, both youths and grey-beards! Some were congregated in groups, conversing and disputing among themselves; others hugged out-of-the-way nooks, away from all the rest. Some (as I clearly perceived, although I dared not speak of it) had eyes but no tongue; others had tongue but no eyes; some had only ears, but no tongue or eyes; and so forth; then I realized that deficiencies existed even here. Seeing that they all issued from a certain place and again re-entered it, like bees swarming in and out of a hive, I prompted my companions to go in as well.

6 DESCRIPTION OF A LIBRARY. So we entered; and behold, a large hall the end of which was out of sight; on all sides were ranged such long rows of shelves, sections, cases, and containers that a hundred thousand wagon loads could not remove them all, and each had its separate designation and title. "What kind of apothecary's shop have we come into, " I inquired. "One which deals in medicines for mind-diseases, " answered my interpreter: "such a place is properly called a libraray. Behold these endless stores of wisdom!" I looked around and watched groups of scholars approaching and handling the equipment. Some selected the best and wittiest, and drawing out a piece, ate it, slowly chewing and digesting it. I went up to one of them and asked him what he was doing. "I am cultivating myself." "And how does the food taste?" "While I am chewing it, " he replied, "it tastes bitter and acrid; but later it turns sweet." "But why are you eating it?" I continued. "I find it more convenient to carry it within, " he answered; " for I am then surer of it. Do you not observe the benefit?" I scrutinized him more carefully and saw that he was stout and fat, with a healthy complexion; his eyes shone like candles, his diction was carefully chosen, and everything about him had an air of livelines. "Look at these!" my interpreter told me.

7 THE EVILS OF STUDIES. I looked and behold! some men behaving very greedily, glutting themselves with anything they could lay their hands on. Observing them more carefully, I noticed that they neither improved their complexion nor gained flesh or fat, save that their belly was blown and swelled out; I also perceived that whatever they crammed in, passed out at both ends undigested. Some of them became dizzy or lost their minds; others grew pallid, pined away, and died. Others seeing this, singled out these men as a warning against the dangers in the use of books (as they called the boxes); thereupon, some ran away; others exhorted all to deal carefully with those things. Hence, these latter did not consume them inwardly, but packed them into sacks or bags which they kept suspended before or behind their persons (for the greatest part, they selected the following titles: the Vocabulary, the Dictionary, the Lexicon, Illustrations, Quotations, Loci communes , Postils, Concordances, Herbaria, and such others as they deemed the most appropriate to their needs) and these they carried about, and whenever they had occasion to speak or write, they drew them out of their pockets and culled out whatever was needed for their tongue or pen. Perceiving this, I said: "I notice that these people carry their knowledge in their pockets." "Those are merely aids to memory, " my interpreter answered; "have you not heard of them?" I have, indeed, heard some praise this custom on the ground that such men brought out only generally approved knowledge. That might very well have been the case. I observed, however, that the custom had this disadvantage. It happened in my presence that some misplaces boxes, while others, having laid them aside, lost them in fire. What running about, wringing of hands, lamenting, and imploring of aid then ensued! For the time being nobody was willing to dispute, or write, or preach; but walking about with downcast eyes, cringing and blushing, he begged or purchased from his acquintances a new outfit; those, however, who had inner store of knowledge, were not afraid of such a mishap.

8 STUDENT WHO DOES NOT STUDY. Moreover, I observed certain of them who did not even trouble themselves to carry the boxes in their pockets, but stored them in their rooms; I followed them and saw that they made beautiful receptacles for the books, painting them various colors, some daubing them with silver and gold; then they placed the books on or took them off the shelves, pleased with looking at them; they continued putting up and taking down the books, approaching or retreating, pointing out to each other or to strangers the excellent appearance of them, all superficially. Some occasionally looked at the titles to memorize the names of the works. "What are these folk playing?" I inquired. "My dear fellow," replied the interpreter, "it is a fine thing to possess a fine library." "Even when it is not used?" I remarked. "Lovers of books are also counted among the learned, " he rejoined. I thought to myself: just as well might a man be counted among blacksmiths if he possessed a heap of hammers and pincers, but did not know how to use them! Nevertheless, I forebore to speak for fear of catching something.

CHAPTER XI

THE PILGRIM CAME AMONG THE PHILOSOPHERS

Then my interpreter addressed me: "Now I shall lead you among the philosophers whose task it is to discover the means of correcting all human deficiencies and to show the essence of true wisdom." "God grant that I shall at last learn something certain," said I. "Of course you will, " he replied; "for these are men who know the truth of everything, without whose knowledge neither heaven manifests itself nor does the abyss hide anything; they guide human life nobly to virtue, enlighten communities and countries, and have God for their friend; for their wisdom penetrates His secrets." "Let us hurry, please, " I urged; "let us go among them as quickly as possible. " But when he brought me among these men, and I saw a crowd of these oldsters with their strange antics, I stood as if petrified. For there Bion sat still, Anacharsis strolled about, Thales flew, Hesiod plowed, Plato chased ideas in the air, Homer sand, Aristotle disputed, Pythagoras kept still, Epimenides slept, Archimedes tried to push the earth away, Solon was composing laws and Galen prescriptions, Euclid was measuring the hall, Cleobulus was peering into the future, Periander was defining duties, Pittacus was waging war, Bias was begging, Epictetus was serving, Seneca, sitting among tons of gold, was extolling poverty, Socrates was confiding to everybody that he knew nothing, Xenophon, on the contrary, was promising to teach everything to everybody, Diogenes, peering out of his barrel, was deriding all passersby, Timon was cursing all, Democritus was laughig at it all, Heraclitus, on the contrary, was weeping, Zeno was fasting, Epicurus was feasting, while Anaxarchus was holding forth that all these things were only apparent, not real. Moreover, there was a flock of smaller philosophical fry, each of whom was doing something extraordinary; but I neither remember nor care to recount it +29all. Observing it all, I said: "Are these, then, the wise men, the light of the world? Alas! Alas! I had hoped for better things! For these act like peasants in a tavern: they all howl, and each to a different tune." "You are a dunce," my interpreter retorted, "you dod not understand such mysteries." Hearing that there were mysteries, I began to scrutinize the crowd meticulously, while my interpreter began to explain them to me. Straightway a man (called Paul of Tarsus) in a philosopher's garb, approached me and whispered into my ear: "If any man among you thinks he is wise in this world, let him become a fool that he may be wise. For the wisdom of the world is but foolishness with God. For it is written: The Lord knows the thoughts of the wise that they are +30futile." Perceiving that what my eyes have seen and my ears have heard agreed with this speech, I willingly acquiesced and said: "Let us go elsewhere." My interpreter scolded me for being such a fool, saying that when I might learn something among the wise, I ran away from them. But I pressed on in silence.

2 HE CAME AMONG THE GRAMMARIANS. We then entered a lecture room full of young and old, who, with pointers in their hands, were engaged in drawing letters, dashes, and +31dots; whenever any of them wrote or pronounced his formula differently from the rest, they either ridiculed or scolded him. Moreover, they hung some words on the wall and disputed as to what belonged to which; then they composed, separated, or transposed them variously. I looked at this for a while, but seeing nothing in it, I said: "These are but childish trivialities. Let us go elsewhere."

3 AMONG THE RHETORICIANS. Thereupon we entered another hall where many were gathered with brushes in their hands, discussing how words, either written or escaping from the mouth into the air, could be painted green, red, black, white, or any other color +32desired. I inquired what the purpose of this procedure. "This is done in order that the hearers' brain may be colored in different ways," my interpreter replied. "Are these disguises intended to bring out truth or falsehood?" I continued. "Either one, " he answered. "Then there is as much fraud and falsehood as truth and benefit in it," I remarked, and went out.

4 AMONG THE POETS. We then entered another place; and behold! a crowd of spry-looking adolescents weighing syllables in scales and arranging them in [metrical] feet, meanwhile rejoicing over their work and skipping +33about. I was amazed and inquired what it all meant. "Of all literary arts, " my interpreter explained, "this one is the most skillful and gay." "But what is it ?" I inquired. "Whatever cannot be managed by simple coloring of the words, " he answered, "is accomplished by this folding process." Noticing that those who were learning this art of word-folding consulted certain books, I also glanced into them and read their titles: De Culice, De Passere, De Lesbia, De Priapo, De arte amandi, Metamorphoses, Encomia, Satirae , or in a word, farces, poems, comedies, and all kinds of other +34frivolities. This made me somehow loathe the whole +35thing. Especially when I perceived that whenever anyone flattered those syllable-mongers, they expended all their art on his adulation; but whenever anyone displeased them, they showered him with sarcasms. Thus the art was used for nothing but flattery or defamation. Discerning what passionate folk they were, I gladly hurried away from them.

5 AMONG THE DIALECTICIANS. Entering another building, we found that lenses for glasses were ground and sold +36there. I inquired what they were. Notiones secundae, they told me. Whoever possessed them could see not only the exterior of things, but to their very core; especially could one look into another's brain, and scrutinize his mind. Many people came to

buy these glasses, and the masters taught them how to put them on and, if need be, to readjust them. There were special master glass-grinders who had their workshops in obscure nooks; but they did not make the glasses identical. One made them lage, another small; one round, another polygonal. Each praised his own wares and tried to attract buyers, while among themselves they quarreled perpetually and heckled each other. Some buyers purchased glasses from each of the makers, and put them all on; others selected and used only one pair. Thereupon some complained that even so they could not penetrate as deeply as they had been told, while others claimed that they could, and pointed to each other beyond the mind and all reason. But I noticed that not a few of these latter, venturing to step out, stumbled over boulders and stumps and fell into ditches, of which, as I had remarked before, the place was full. "How does it happen, " I asked, "that although everything may be seen through the glasses, these people do not avoid the obstacles?" I was told that it was not the fault of the glasses, but of the people who did not know who to use them. The masters added, moreover, that it was not sufficient to possess the glasses of dialectic, but that the eyes must be cleared with the bright eye-salve of physics and mathematics. Therefore, they advised the buyers to repair to the other halls and to have their eyesight improved. Accordingly, they went, one here, another there. Thereupon, I said to my guides: "Let us follow as well." We did not go, however, until at the prompting of Mr. Searchall I had procured and put on several pairs of these glasses. It is true that I seemed able to discern somewhat more than before, and that a particular thing could be seen from several points of view. But still I insisted that we proceed to the place where I could try the eye-salve of which they had spoken.

6 AMONG THE NATURAL SCIENTISTS. So we went, and they led me to a certain square in the center of which I saw a large, wide-spreading tree bearing diversely-shaped leaves and various fruit (all in hard shells); they called it Nature. A large number of philosophers had gathered around, examining it and explaining to each other what the name of each branch, leaf, or fruit was. "These, I hear, are learning the names of these things, " I said, "but I do not perceive that they apprehend their real being." "Not every one is able to do that, " my interpreter anwered; "nevertheless, watch these men here. " I saw some of them break off the branches and open the leaves and the shell, and finding the nut, cracking it with such a force that they well-nigh broke their teeth: but they claimed to have broken the shells; then picking over the crushed mass, they boasted to have discovered the kernel, and surreptitiously showed it to a select few among the company. But when I diligently scrutinized the procedure, I perceived plainly that although they had indeed broken the outer husk and the integuement, the inner hard shell, containing the kernel, remained whole. Being thus aware of their immodest boasts and futile toil (for some of them had lost their sight and broken their teeth) I suggested that we go elsewhere.

7 AMONG THE METAPHYSICIANS. Thereupon, we entered another hall; and lo! it was full of philosophical gentlemen who were examining cows, asses, wolves, serpents, and various other beasts, birds, reptiles, as well as wood, stone, water, fire, clouds, stars, planets, and indeed even the angels; thereupon, they held disputations among themselves as to how each creature could be deprived of its distinctive characteristics so that all might become +37alike. They first divested them of their form, then of their substance, and finally of all their "accidents", until nothing but the "being" remained. Then they quarreled whether all these things were one and the same; or whether they were all good; or whether they really were what they appeared to be; and about many other similar questions. Some of those observing them expressed their amazement at the surpassing keenness of the human wit that was able to fathom the essence of all things and to divest all corporeal beings of their corporeality; indeed, I myself began to be fascinated by these subtleties. Just then, however, a man stepped out, crying that all these studies were but fantasies, and exhorted all to abandon +38them. Thereupon, some were indeed drawn after him. But others rose up and condemned them as heretics, accusing them of wishing to deprive philosophy of its highest art and, as it were, of decapitating knowledge. Having listened sufficiently to these wranglings, I went away.

CHAPTER XII

THE PILGRIM EXAMINES ALCHEMY

Thereupon, Mr. Ubiquitous remarked: "Now come along, for I shall take you to a place where you will find the highest peak of human ingenuity, and show you an occupation so delightful that anyone who has once turned to it is never again willing to abandon it as long as he lives, because of the charm and delight which it affords his mind." I begged him not to delay in showing me. Thereupon he led me down into some cellars where I saw several rows of fireplaces, small ovens, kettles, and glass instruments, all shining brightly. Men tending the fires were gathering and piling on brushwood and blowing into it, or again extinguishing it, filling and pouring something from one glass into another. "Who are these folk, and what are they doing?" I asked. "They are the most ingenious of philosophers," my interperter answered, "effecting instantly what the celestial sun with its heat can effect in the bowels of the earth only after a considerable number of years: they transform various metals into their highest category, namely, gold." "But for what purpose, " I asked, "since iron and other metals are of more frequent use than gold?" "What a dunce you are!" he exclaimed, "don't you know that gold is the most precious of metals, and that he who has gold need fear no poverty?

2 LAPIS PHILOSOPHICUS*. "Besides, that which has the potency to change metals into gold possesses other most astounding properties: for instance, it can preserve human health to the end of life, and ward off death for two or three hundred years. In fact, if men knew how to use it, they could make themselves immortal. For this stone is nothing less than the seed of life, the kernel and the quintessence of the universe, from which all animals, plants, metals, and the very elements derive their being." I was affrighted, hearing such astounding news, and asked: "Are these people, then, immortal?" "Not all are so fortunate as to discover the stone, " he answered, "and those who find it do not alwasys know how to use it effectively." "If I had the stone, " I remarked, "I would take care to use it in such a way as to keep death away, and would procure plenty of gold for myself and others. But where is the stone to be found?" "It is prepared here, " he answered. "In these small kettles?" I exclaimed. "Yes."

3 THE MISHAPS OF THE ALCHEMISTS. Full of curiosity, I walked about scrutinizing everything to learn what and how the thing was done; but I observed that not all fared equally. The fire of one was not hot enough: his mixture did not reach the boiling point. Another had too intense a fire, and his glass retorts cracked and something puffed out. As he explained it, the nitrogen had escaped; and he wept. Another, while pouring the liquid, spilled it or mixed it wrongly. Another burned his eyes out, and was thus unable to supervise the calcination and the fixation: or bleared his sight with smoke to such an extent that before he cleared his eyes the nitrogen escaped. Some died of asphyxiation from the smoke. But for the greatest part they did not have enough coal in their bags and were obliged to run about to borrow it elsewhere, while in the meantime their concoction cooled off and was utterly ruined. This was of very frequent, in fact of almost constant, occurrence. Although they did not tolerate anyone among themselves save such as possessed full bags, yet these seemed to have a way of drying up very rapidly, and soon grew empty: they were obliged either to suspend their operations or to run away to borrow.

4 After watching them, I said: "I see a good many here toil vain; but perceive none who succeeds in getting the stone. I also see that these people boil and burn both their gold and their lives, and often squander and burn both; but where are those with the heaps of gold and immortality?" "Naturally, they do not reveal themselves to you, " my interpreter answered, "nor would I advise them so to do. Such a priceless thing must be kept secret. For if one of the rulers learned of such a man, he would immediately demand his surrender and the poor fellow would become no better than a prisoner for life; consequently, them must keep themselves in hiding."

5 Then I observed some of the scorched ones gather together, and turning my ear toward them, I heard them discuss the causes of their failures. One blamed the philosophers for their too involved description of the art; another lamented the brittleness of the glass implements; a third complained of an untimely and inauspicious aspect of the planets; a fourth was disgruntled with the earthly impurities of the mercury; a fifth complained of lack of capital. In short, there were so many causes of failure that I saw that they were at a loss to know how to mend their art. Thus when they left one after another, I left also.

CHAPTER XIII

THE PILGRIM OBSERVES THE ROSICRUCIANS

FAMA FRATERNITATIS, ANNO 1612 LATINE AC GERMANICE EDITA*. Then I heard in the square the blare of a trumpet, and turning back I perceived a rider on horseback, calling the philosophers together. When a crowd of them gathered about him from all sides, he began to harangue them in five languages about the imperfections of the liberal arts and of philosophy generally. He announced that certain famous men, impelled by God, had ascertained and corrected all such imperfections, and restored the wisdom of mankind to the same degree of perfection which it had had in paradise before the Fall. To make gold, he said, is the least among hundreds of their accomplishments: for all nature stands naked and uncovered before them and they are able to transfer at pleasure the form of any creature to another. They know the languages of all nations, and are aware of all that is taking place everywhere in the world, including the New World, and are able to discourse among themselves even though they be thousands of miles apart. They also possess the [philosophers'] stone, with which they are able to heal perfectly all kinds of diseases, and to impart long life. Thus, for example, their president, Hugo Alverda, had attained the age of five hundred and sixty-two years, and his colleagues not much less. And although they have kept themselves hidden for so many hundreds of years, during which time seven of them devoted themselves to the improvement of philosophy, they have now, at last, brought it all to perfection. Moreover, knowing that the reformation of the whole world is about to begin, they wish no longer to keep themselves in hiding, but announce quickly their willingness to share their priceless secrets with anyone whom they should recognize as being worthy. If any such makes himself known to them, be he of whatever language or nationality, they will learn of it, and no one will be left without a kindly answer. However, if any unworthy person should apply from motives of avarice or idle curiosity, such a person will not be able to learn anything about them.

2 VARIA DE FAMA* JUDICIA. Having finished his speech, the herald disappeared; looking about me at the learned, I saw them well-nigh terrified by the news. Gradually they began to put their heads together and to express their judgement about the matter, some in whispers, others aloud. Joining a group here and there, I listened: some were exceedingly glad, hardly knowing how to contain themselves for joy. They pitied their ancestors whose age had afforded them nothing comparable, and considered themselves blessed to be so freely offered a perfect philosophy: to know everything infallibly, to possess everything in abundance, and to live several hundred years without sickness or grey hairs--all to be had by anyone desiring it! They kept on repeating: "Happy, thrice happy, is our age!" Hearing thees words, I myself began to rejoice, indulging in the hope of sharing, God willing, the blessings upon which the others were counting. But I saw others buried in deep thought, greatly perplexed what to think of the news. They wished it were true, but the matter appeared to them dubious and surpassing human reason. Others openly rejected it, declaring it to be a fraud and a deceit. "If these men have lived for so many centuries, " they said, "why have they not revealed themselves sooner? If they are so sure of their cause, why do they not step out freely into the light, instead of squeaking like bats out of some obscure nook? Philosophy is well enough established and needs no reformation; should we allow it to be snatched out of our hands, we shall be left without any." Others even heaped terrible scoffing and abuse upon them, denouncing them as diviners, sorcerers, and demons incarnate.

3 FRATERNITATEM AMBIENTES**. In short, the whole square was filled with clamor, and almost all burned with the desire to reach the fraternity. Therefore, not a few of them wrote their supplications, some secretly, others openly, and sent them off, full of joy in anticipation of being received into the fraternity. But I perceived that after the supplications had gone to every conceivable nook, all were returned unanswered. Then their joyful hope was turned into grief: besides, they had to endure jeers of the sceptics. Some wrote another petition, and then a second, a third or even more, begging and imploring, in the name of all the Muses and in the most affecting manner, that the fraternity decline not a mind a thirst for knowledge. Some, impatient of delay, personally undertook the journey from one end of the world to the other, but lamented their misfortune in not being able to find those happy folk. Some ascribed the reason for their failure to their own unworthiness, others to the ill-will of the fraternity. Consequently, some fell into despair, while others tortured themselves by persisting in their endeavo to discover ever new ways of ascertaining the group's whereabouts, until I myself grew weary of waiting for the final outcome.

4 CONTINUATIO Then a trumpet blared again: when many ran out to find out what the sound imported, I joined them also. I saw a m an setting up a booth, inviting the bystanders to examine and to buy his most wonderful mysteries; he claimed to have taken them from the treasures of the new philosophy, and assured all desirous of the secert wisdom would find satisfaction therein. Then many rejoiced that the holy Brotherhood of the Rose had openly and liberally shared its treasures and approaching, bought the wares. All articles put up for sale were enclosed in painted boxes, bearing attractive inscriptions such as: Good Guide to the Large and the Small Cosmos; A Harmony of the Two Worlds; The Christian Cabala; The Case of Nature; The Castle of Primordial Matter; The Divin Magic; The General Tri-Trinity; The Triumphal Pyramid; Hallelujah; and so forth. But the buyers were forbidden to open the boxes. For the efficacy of the secret wisdom was said to be so powerful that

it operated by penetration, and would evaporate if the box were opened. Nevertheless, some of the more inquisitive could not refrain from opening their boxes and found them entirely empty! Thereupon, they showed them to others, who also opened their boxes and likewise found nothing. Then they raised a cry of "Fraud! Fraud!" and assaulted the dealer with fury. He attempted to pacify them by saying that the most secret part of the mystery consisted in the fact that these things were invisible to all save the sons of science; and since barely one out of a thousand possessed the proper qualifications, he, the dealer, was not to blame for it.

5 EVENTUS FAMAE. The buyers for the greatest part were pacified thereby; in the meantime the dealer packed up his wares, while the spectators dispersed in very different humors, one here, another there. But whether or not anyone had discovered the new mysteries, I have hitherto been unable to learn. This only I know that thereafter everything quieted down and those who had been formerly running and rushing about the most, were found sitting in obscure corners with their mouths shut. Either they had been (as some thought) admitted to the mysteries upon an oath that theyleep them secret; or (as it appeared to me observing them from under my glasses) were ashamed of their blasted hopes and misspent effort. Thus everything passed and quieted down as clouds disperse after a rainless storm. I said to my companions: "Are all these things, then, an utter failure? Oh, my disappointed hopes! Hearing such boastful promises, I expected to find a profitable pasture for my mind." My interpreter answered: "Who knows but it might yet materialize? Perhaps they know their hoiur when and to whom to reveal themselves." "Should I wai for such an event, when I have not seen a single instance of success among so many thousands of men more learned than I am? I do not care to gape any longer: let us go away," I said.

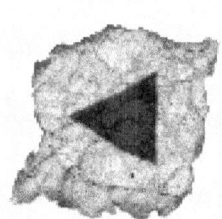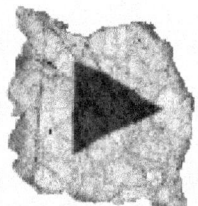

CHAPTER XIV

THE PILGRIM EXAMINES THE MEDICAL PROFESSION

ANATOMY. Having been conducted through some alleys between the physics and the chemistry lecture rooms into another square, I beheld a gruesome sight. There men stretched out a corpse before them and cutting off one limb after another, examined the viscera, with keen relish exhibiting to each other what they +50found. "What cruelty to deal with a human being as if he were a beast!" I exclaimed. "It must be done; this is their school, " my interpreter replied.

2 BOTANY. Thereupon, abandoning that task and dispersing into gardens, meadows, fields, and mountains, they plucked whatever they found growing there and piled it into such heaps that many years would scarcely suffice for its mere sorting and scanning. Then each snatched from the heap what he saw fit or happened to lay his hand on and running to the ripped-up body, measured it with the limbs as to their length, width, and thickness. One said that it fitted; another denied it. Then they shouted at each other in dispute; they had great controversies about the very names of the herbs. He who knew the greatest number of them and how to measure and weight them, was crowned with a wreath of those herbs, and was to be called the doctor of the art.

3 PRAXIS MEDENDI. Then I saw a number of wounded, both externally and internally, with putrid and rotting limbs, brought or conducted to the physicians; they approached them, examined the putrifications, smelling the stench emitted from them, and scrutinized the evacuations proceeding from both above and below, until the sight was disgusting; this they called diagnosis. Then they cooked, steamed, roasted, broiled, cauterized, cooled, burned, hacked, sawed, stabbed, sewed again, bound, annointed, hardened, softened, wrapped, or moistened, and I know not what more they did in oder to effect the cure. In the meantime, their patients had been expiring under their hands, not a few of them lamenting the doctors' ignorance or carelessness as the causes of their death. In a word, I saw that although the art of these fine salve-mongers brought them a certain gain, it also involved them, on the other hand (if they wished to do justice to their calling), in a great deal of very strenuous and partly even disgusting labor, and in the end brought them as much blame as praise. This made it distasteful to me.

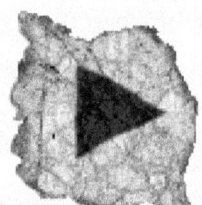

CHAPTER XV

THE PILGRIM OBSERVES THE LEGAL PROFESSION

FINIS JURIS. In the last place, they led me into still another very spacious lecture room where I saw a greater number of distinguished men than anywhere else. The walls around were painted with stone walls, barriers, picket-fences, plank-fences, bars, rails, and gate staves, interspersed at various intervals by gaps and holes, doors and gates, bolts and locks, and along with it larger and smaller keys and hooks. All this they pointed out to each other, measuring where and how one might or might not pass through. "What are these people doing?" I inquired. I was told that they were searching for means how every man in the world might hold his own or might also peacefully obtain something from another's property without disturbing order and concord. "That is a fine thing!" I remarked. But observing it a while, it grew disgusting to me.

2 JUS CIRCA QUID VESETUR. For, in the first place, I noticed that the barriers enclosed neither the soul, the mind, nor the body of man, but solely his property, which is of incidental importance to him; and it did not seem to me worthy of the extremely difficult toil that was, as I saw, expended upon it.

3 FUNDAMENTUM JURIS. Besides, I observed that all this science was founded upon the mere whim of a few men to whom one or another thing seemed worthy of being enjoined as a statute and which the others now obsesrved. Moreover (as I noticed here), some erected or demolished the bars or gaps as the notion entered their heads. Consequently, there was much outright contradiction in it all, the rectification of which caused a group of them a great deal of curious and ingenious labor; I was amazed that the;y sweated and toiled so much upon most insignificant minutiae, amounting to very little, and occurring scarcely once in a millenium; and all with not a little pride. For the more a man broke through some bar or made an opening that he was able to wall up again, the better he thought of himself and the more was he envied by others. But some (in order to show the keenness of their wit) rose up and opposed him, contending that the bars should be set up or the gaps broken thus so. Hence arose contentions and quarrels, until finally separating, they painted each his case in his own way, at the same time attracting spectators to themselves. Observing this tomfoolery sufficiently, I shook my head, exclaiming: "Let us hurry away! I feel distressed here!" "Is there anything in the world to your liking?" my interpreter angrily retorted. "You find fault even with the noblest of callings, you weathercock!" "It seems that he is religious-minded; let us take him to see the clerical professions; perhaps he will find it to his liking, " Mr. Ubiquitous suggested.

  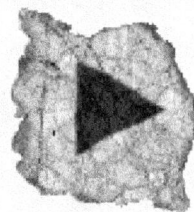

CHAPTER XVI

THE PILGRIM OBSERVES THE PROMOTION OF MASTERS AND DOCTORS

But behold! a trumpet sounded as if summoning the people for a celebration; Mr. Searchall, divining what was to happen, suggested: "Let us return for a moment; there will be something worth seeing." "What will it be?" I inquired. He answered: "The Academy is going to crown those who, having exercised superior diligence, have attained the summit of learning; these, I say, are to be crowned as an example to all others." Desirous to see such a rare spectacle, and seeing the multitudes rushing thither, I followed after the crowd; here, under the "philosophical +51sky, " stood a personage holding a paper sceptre, to whom some from among the crowd presented themselves, requesting an attestation of their high learning. He approved their request as proper and commanded them to present in writing what they knew and to which they desired certification. Thereupon one expounded a summary of philosophy; another , of medicine; another, of law; but at the same time, in order to make the progress smoother, they greased the way with their purses.

2 The personage then, taking the candidates ones by one, pasted a title on their foreheads: this is a Master of Liberal Arts; this is a Doctor of Medicine; this is a Licentiate of Both Laws, +52etc. Then he confirmed these titles with his seal, and commanded all, whether present or absent, on pain of the disfavor of the goddess Pallas Athene, not to address them otherwise, when they met them, except by those titles. Therewith he dismissed both them and the multitude. "Is there something more to follow?" I asked. "Isn't that enough for you?" retorted my interpreter. "Don't you see how everybody gives way before them?" And indeed, they did give way.

3 However, wishing to learn how they fared afterwards, I observe one of those masters of arts: they asked him to figure out something, he could not; to measure something, he could not; to name the stars, he could not; to make syllogisms, he could not; to speak in foreign languages, he could not; to deliver an oration in his own tongue, he could not; at last they bade him read and write, but he could not. "What a shame, " I exclaimed, "to subscribe oneself a master of the seven arts but to know none of them!" "If this one does not know them, " my interpreter answered, "another or a third or fourth does; all cannot be equally proficient." "Do I understand, then, " I replied, "that after one has spent his youth and his substance in schools, after he has been loaded with titles and seals, it is necessary to ask whether he has learned anything? May God save us from such a pass!" "You will never cease playing the wiseacre, " he retorted, "until you catch something! Just keep on babbling like that, and I swear that you will surely suffer for it. " "Well, then, " I replied, "even if they be masters or doctos of seventy-seven arts, and know them all or none, I will not say a word; only let us go away."

CHAPTER XVII

THE PILGRIM EXAMINES THE RELIGIOUS PROFESSION

THE PAGANS. Thereupon they led me through some passages from which we emerged upon a square full of churches and chapels of different architectures. Multitudes kept going in and out of them. We stepped into the nearest and lo! there were pictures and statues of men and women on all sides, as well as of all kinds of animals, birds, reptiles, tress, and plants; likewise of the sun, the moon, the stars, and of many ugly demons. Each of those entering this place chose whatever pleased him best and kneeling before it, kissed it, burning incense or a sacrifice before it. I was amazed at the concord among them, for in spite of the ritual differences, they tolerated them all, and peacefully allowed everyone to keep his own opinion (a practice I have not since seen elsewhere); being assailed by an overpowering stench, I was seized with terror; so I soon hastened out.

2 THE JEWS. We then entered another temple, white and clean, containing nothing but living images; these, wagging their heads, mumbled something in a low voice; or arising and stopping up their ears, they opened their mouths wide and gave out sounds not unlike those of howling wolves. TALMUDI FIGMENTA*. Then they gathered themselves together to examine certain books; approaching closer, I saw in them bizarre illustrations. For instance, feathered and winged beasts and wingless birds; beasts with human and men with beastlike limbs; one body with many heads and one head with many bodies; some of these monsters had a head in place of the tail and a tail in place of the head; some had eyes on the belly and feet on their backs: some had ears, mouths, and feet without number, while others had none. Everything was strangely transposed, twisted, inverted, and perverted, as well as greatly out of proportion: one limb was a foot long, another a rod in length; one was a finger's width, another a barrel's; in a word, all was monstrous beyond belief. But they, claiming all this to be historically correct, praised it as excellent, and the older exhibited it to the young as a mystery. "Who would have imagined that there would exist folk who actually relish such unappetizing things, " I remarked. "Let us go elsewhere, leaving them alone." We went out, and I noticed these people mingling with the rest; however, they were disliked by all others and were the target of their jests and pranks. This inclined me to disdain them.

3 THE MOSLEMS. We then entered another temple, which was round, and although not inferior in beauty to the former, was without any ornaments; save some lettering on the walls and carpets on the floor. The worshippers, all clad in white, behaved quietly and reverently, they were great lovers of cleanliness and were constantly performing ablutions, and distributing alms, so on account of their external appearance I began to feel favorably inclined toward them. "What is the foundation of their belief?" I inquired. "They carry it hidden under their robes," Mr. Searchall answered. I approached closer and begged to see it. But they replied that it was not proper for anyone but their interpreters to examine it. I persisted in my request, adducing the permission of the Lord Fate in my behalf.

4 A SUMMARY OF THE KORAN. Finally they took out and showed me a chart upon which a tree was depicted with its roots up in the air and its branches stuck in the ground; many moles, supervised by a large mole who was running about, calling the others and assigning them their several tasks, were busy digging around this tree. They told me that the branches of the tree underground bore all kinds of delicious fruit which the silent and industrious little creatures brought to light. "And that is, " explained Mr. Searchall, "the sum of their religion." I understood therefrom that its foundation rests upon the wind of supposition and its goal and fruit consist in burrowing in the ground and rejoicing over invisible delights which do not exist, and seeking blindly they know not what.

5 MUHAMMEDANISM IS FOUNDED ON FORCE. Leaving the place, I remarked to my guide: "How do they prove that this really is a reliable and true foundation of religion?" "Come and see!" he replied. We passed behind the temple into a square where we saw those white-clad and well-washed folk rolling up their sleeves and with fire in their eyes, biting their lips and roaring terribly, rushing about and putting to the sword anyone whom they encountered as they waded in human blood. I was terrified and ran back, exclaiming: "What are they doing?" "They are disputing about religion and proving that the Koran is true, " they answered me

6 PERSIANS AND TURKS QUARREL ABOUT THE KORAN. We re-entered the temple and there witnesses a controversy among those who carried the chart concerning, as I understood, the chief mole. One party claimed that he alone was directing those smaller moles, while the other party contended that he had two helpers. This question involved them in such an interminable struggle that in the end they fought with sword and fire both among themselves and with those outside, until it was terrible to behold.

CHAPTER XVIII

HE EXAMINES THE CHRISTIAN RELIGION

Seeing my fright, my guide said to me: "Let us go then. I will show you the Christian religion, which, being founded upon reliable divine relevations, beautifully agrees with itself and benefits both the simplest and the most learned. It exhibits clearly and lucidly the heavenly truth and refutes all opposing erroneous fictions. Its ornaments are concord and love. And having overcome innumerable tribulations, it has remained and shall ever remain unconquered. From this you may readily understand that its origin must be from God, and consequently you shall be able to find in it true solace." Hearing such a speech, I was filled with joy. Thus we went on.

BAPTISM. When we approached nearer, I perceived a gate through which all who wished to enter were obliged to pass. This gate stood in water, through which every applicant must wade and in which he must washe himself, receiving thereupon a badge, white and red in color. Moreover, he must take an oath to observe their laws and regulations, to believe as they do, pray as they do, and keep their ordinances as they do. I was much pleased with this; for it seemed like the beginning of a noble order.

PREACHING THE GOSPEL. Having passed through the gate, I beheld a great multitude of people among whom some were distinguished by their garb from the rest; they were standing on platforms here and there, exhibiting a picture so artistically painted that the more one observed it the more the he found to note. But since the picture was not highly embellished with gold and brilliant colors, it was not clearly visible from a distance. Hence, I noticed that those who stood afar were not greatly allured by its beauty, while those standing nearer could never look at if sufficiently.

4 THE IMAGE OF CHRIST. Those who exhibited this portrait extolled it exceedingly, calling it the Son of God. They professed to find all the most excellent virtues depicted in it; they said that it had been sent into the world from heaven that men might know how to order their own virtues by following it as an example. Thereupon, there arose great rejoicing and exultation among the multitude who, falling on their knees, lifted up their hands to heaven and praised God for it. Seeing this, I also united my voice with theirs and praised the Almighty God for having brought me to this place.

5 SPIRITUAL FEASTS OF CHRISTIANS. In the meantime I heard many and various exhortations, urging all to conform themselves to the portraits. I also observed that those who had been entrusted with the care of the picture gathered themselves at several places and making a small likeness of it, distributed it to all in a kind of wrapping. People then reverently placed it in their mouths. I inquired what this ritual meant and was told that it was not sufficient to look upon the picture outwardly, but that it must likewise be received internally in order that one might be transformed into its beauty. For this heavenly medicine was said to remove sins. Being satisfied with this explanation, I extolled the Christians within myself as blessed among men for possessing such means and aids for the banishing of evil.

LICENTIOUSNESS OF CHRISTIANS. But in the meantime, observing a few who had just a short time before received their god into themselves (as they expressed it), I saw that one after another they gave themselves up to drinking bouts, brawls, uncleanness, and robbery. Not believing my eyes, I watched them more closely and saw in very truth that they got drunk and vomited, quarrelled and fought, defrauded and stole from one another by might and main, neighed and leaped into their license, screamed and shouted, indulged in adultery and fornificatio even worse than any other group I have ever observed. In short, they did everything contrary to the exhortations they had received and the promises they had made. I was deeply grieved by this and exclaimed sorrowfully: "In God's name, what is happening here? I sought here better things!" "Do not express your astonishment so rudely, " my interpreter reproved me, "that which is presented to men for imitation is a degree of perfection that human frailty does not allow every one to attain; the leaders are more perfect; the ordinary man, however, being held back by his evil propensities, is not able to keep up with them." "Let us go among the leaders, then," I suggested, " that I may see them."

7 BARRENNESS OF PREACHERS. Thereuponn, they led me to those who were standing on the platform, exhorting people to admire the beauty of the picture. Nevertheless, they acted somewhat feebly, it seemed to me: for if anyone obeyed them and followed, well and good; if not, it did not matter. A few among them jingled some keys, claiming the power of locking the gate to God to those who would refuse to obey, but as a matter of fact locking it to none; and if they did, it was done in jest. I saw, indeed, that they dared not to do it freely; for if any of the preachers assumed a sharper tone, he was immediately loudly denounced as preaching against individuals. Thus when they could not rebuke sins by the word of mouth, some attempted

to do it in writing. But they were dencounced as broadcasting lampoons. People either turned away from them so as not to hear them or threw them down from the platform, setting up more moderate preachers in their stead. Seeing this, I exclaimed: "What a folly to make mere followers and flatteres of their leaders and counsellors!" "Such is the course of the world, " replied my interpreter; "and it does no harm. If those howlers had full liberty, who knows what they would not dare. Even they must be shown where the limits are."

CARNALITY OF THE CLERGY. "Let us go among them, then, " I said, "that I may see how they manage their affairs at home, out of their pulpits. I know that there at leaset no one domineers over them or interferes with them." We entered a building occupied exclusively by priests. I expected to find them at prayers or delving into the mysteries; but on the contrary, I found them lying on feather beds and snoring, or seated behind tables and feasting, gorging themselves with food and drink to speechlessness; some were dancing and skipping about; others were engaged in stuffing their purses, coffers, and treasure-chambers; some indulged in lechery and wantonness; others spent their time in putting on spurs, daggers, rapiers, and muskets; yet others in hunting hares with dogs. They spent the least of their time with the Bible, some scarcely ever taking it into their hands, and yet called themselves teachers of the Word! Seeing this, I exclaimed: "O my grief! Are these supposed to be the leaders to heaven and the examples of virtue? Shall I ever find an;ything in the world free from falsehood and deceit?" Hearing my exclamation, some of the priests perceived my criticism of their irregularities and began to look askance at me and to grumble: that if I were looking for hypocrites and a show of sanctimoniousness, I must look elsewhere; that they knew how to perform their duty both i church and at home, and how to conduct themselves among men manfully. Thus I was reduced to silence, plainly perceiving, however, that to wear a coat of mail over the surplice and a helmet over the biretta was a monstrosity; the Law in one hand, a sword in the other; Peter's keys in front, Judas' bag behind; the mind trained in Scripture, the heart practiced in fraud; the tongue full of piety, the eyes full of wantonness.

9 WITH HEAVENLY GIFTS, THEY HELP OTHERS BUT NOT THEMSELVES. I noticed particularly that some whose sermons were extremely eloquent and full of piety, who were regardedby others as well as by themselves with as great a regard as if they were angels fallen from heaven, yet lived dissolutely as the rest. I could not restrain myself from exclaiming: "Behold, pipes through which good things are conducted, but to which none of the good adheres!" "Even that is a gift of God to be able to preach eloquently about the things of God, " remarked by interpreter. "Indeed it is a gift of God, " I retorted; "but should a man stop with words?"

TRANGRESSIONS OF THE BISHOPS. Meanwhile, perceiving that all these priests had elders above them, called bishops, archbishops, abbots, priors, deans, superintendents, inspectors, etc., who were men of a serious mien and distinction, and who enjoyed general esteem, I thought to myself: Why do they not keep those in the lower ranks in order? Desiring to discover the reason, I followed one of these men into his room, and then a second, a third, a fourth, and so on. I saw that they were so overburdened with work that they could not spare time for supervision. Their occupation, not to mention all the work which they had in common with their clergy, consisted of keeping account of the revenues and the ecclesiastical treasures (as they called it). "I suppose that it is by mistake that they are not called fathers of profits, rather than of +59prophets, " I remarked. "Somebody must take care of the goods which God has bestowed upon the Church, so that they and the endowments of pious forefathers would not be dissipated, " my interpreter answered.

ACTS 6. s Just then one of their number, a man with two keys suspended from his belt--they called him Peter--stepped out and said: "Men and brethren, it is not seemly that we should forsake the Word of God and serve tables and coffers. Let us select, therefore, men of good report, and appoint them over this business: but let us be diligent in prayers and the ministration of the +60Word." Hearing this, I rejoiced, for according to my notion this was good advice. But none of those addressed was willing thus to understand it: all persisted in counting, receiving, and disbursing, while the prayers and the ministry of the Word were either entrusted to others or attended to only perfunctorily.

CHAPTER XIX

THE PILGRIM EXAMINES THE GOVERNING CLASS

THE DIVERS RANK OF NOTABLES. We then entered another street where I saw on all sides a great number of high and low seats, and heard the occupants addressed as the honorable constable, the honorable mayor, the honorable burgomaster, the honorable magistrate, the honorable regent, his lordship the burgrave, his lordship the chancellor, his lordship the viceregent, the honorable judges, his grace the king, or the count, or the lord, and so forth. "Here you see men who pass judgements and sentences in lawsuits, punishing the evil-doers, protecting the good, and thus preserving order in the world, " my interpreter remarked. "This is indeed a splendid thing, and no doubt for mankind a necessary one, " I replied, "but where do such people come from?" "Some are born to their office, " he answered, "while others are selected either by the former, or by their communities, being acknowledged as the wisest and the most experienced of all and the best versed in justice and the laws." "That is also splendid, " I said.

2 Just then my attention was attracted to some who were acquiring seats by bribery, or by importunate solicitation, of by flattery, while some seated themselves therein by force. Seeing this, I cried out: "Look, look, the corruption!" "Keep still, you interfering fool!" warned my interpreter, "or if they should hear you, you would catch it!" "But why do they not wait till they are elected?" I expostulated. "Well, what of it?" he retorted; "doubtless they are confident of being equal to the task. Moreover, as long as others accept them as such, what business is it of yours?"

3 Thereupon, I kept still, and adjusting my glasses, I observed them closely. Thus scrutinizing them, I made an unexpected discovery; for scarcely a single one of them possessed all bodily organs, but each lacked some most necessary limb. Some had no ears with which to hear the grievances of the subjects; others lacked eyes to perceive the evils about them; others lacked the nose wherewith to scent the machinations of crooks plotting against the law; others lacked the tongue with which to defend the mute, oppressed masses; others lacked arms with which to enforce the pronouncements of justice; many even lacked the heart to dare to act in accordance with the dictates of justice.

4 Those, however, who possessed all their bodily organs appeared to me greatly harassed; for they were constantly importuned by petitioners, so that they could hardly eat or sleep in peace. The former, on the contrary, spent more than half of their time in idleness. "But why is law and justice entrusted to people who lack the necessarily bodily organs for the task?" I queried. My interpreter retorted that it was not so, that it only appeared so to me. "For," he said, "whoever knows not how to feign knows not how to rule. He who rules others must often see not, hear not, and understand not, even though he does in fact see, hear, and understand. But you, being inexperienced in politics, cannot understand these things." "Nevertheless, in truth I perceive clearly that they do not possess what they should have, " I persisted. "As to that, I advise you to keep still, " he replied; "otherwise I promise you that unless you cease your impertinent cavils you shall find yourself where you scarcely wish to be. Do you not know that contempt of court is a capital offense?" Thereupon I kept still, but observed all quietly. However, it does not seem necessary to narrate all I saw concerning each of the seats. I shall touch upon but two incidents.

5 FREQUENT TRANSGRESSIONS AND INJUSTICE AMONG JUDGES. I tarried and observed very diligently the procedure in the senatorial court, and learned that the names of the judges were as follows: Atheist, Lovestrife, Hearsayjudge, Partisan, Personrespecter, Lovegold, Bribetake, Tyro, Knowlittle, Dontcare, Hasty, and Anyhow; the President and the Supreme Justice, or Primate, was my Lord Icommandit . I instantly surmised from their names what kind of judges they were like to be; and soon in my presence a case came up which confirmed my surmise. Sincerity was charged by Adversary with having slandered some good people by calling usurers misers, tipplers drunkards, and I do not know what else. The witnesses brought against her were Gossip, Lie, and Suspicion; the prosecuting attorney was named Flatterer, and the counsel for the accused was Prattler, whose services, however, Sincerity declined as unnecessary. Having been asked whether she pleaded guilty [to the charge], she replied: I do , your honors." And she added: "Here I stand; I cannot do otherwise; so help me God!" The judges gathered to cast their votes. Atheist remarked: "What that hussy says is indeed true; but what business is it of hers to babble about it? If we allow her to go one, she will perhaps not spare even us her tongue lashing. I favor her punishment." "Why, of course!" Lovestrife then spoke up, "for if one of them escaped the penalty, others would claim the same immunity!" "Although I really do not know what has happened, " Hearsay judge remarked, "since Adversary ascribes so much importance to the matter, I surmise that he really considers himself injured. Let her be punished. " "I knew in advance that that shrew would blurt out all she knows!" Partisan said, "she needs to have her mouth stopped." "The plaintiff is a good friend of mine, " Personrespecter assented; "she should have spared him at least for my sake, instead of scoffing at him like that. She is worthy of punishment." "You all know how generous Adversary has shown himself; he is worthy of defense, " Lovegold said. "That is what I say, " Bribetake concurred; "we would show ourselves ungrateful, were his suit lost." "I do not know of a similar case; let

her suffer whatever she deserves, " Tyro said. "I do not understand the matter; I agree with your judgement, whatever it is, " Knowlittle added. "Whichever you decide, I agree to it, " Anyhow assented. "Would it not be better to postpone the sentence?" Dontcare queried. "The case might decide itself." "No, no, let the sentence be passed while we are so minded!" Hasty exclaimed. "Why, of course, why shouldwe consider anybody else?" the President agreed. "Whatever justice demands, must be done." Then rising, he delivered the sentence: "Whereas the prattling gossip has given herself to such disreputable conduct as to slander good men, we decree that she suffer, for the taming of her unbridled tongue and as a warning unto others, the punishment of forty slaps in her face save one." Thereupon Adversary with the prosecuting attorney and the witnesses, bowing, thanked the judges for their just sentence. Sincerity was urged to do likewise; but she broke into tears and the wringing of hands. Thereupon, for not having rendered honor to the court, her penalty was increased; and seizing her, they led her away to punishment. Seeing that she had been wronged, I could not restrain myself from crying aloud: "If all the courts in the world are like this one, may the Almighty God help me neither to become a judge, nor to have a litigation with anyone!" "Keep still, you raving maniac, " my interpreter cr

6 PERVERSITY OF LAWYERS. When I stopped outside the court house to catch my breath and to clear my eyes, I noticed many bringing their law-suits to the court; moreover, I preceived that a numbe of lawyers (whose names were Babbler, Flatterer, Leadamiss, Prolongsuit, and such) ran to meet them, offering the litigants their services. They did not inquire about the cases, but first examined the litigant's purses. Each lawyer carried with him his own statutes--which thing I had not noticed among the theologians--and diligently searched therein. I got a glimpse of the title of some of the copies, which read,The Rapacious Gnawing of the Land, and The Voracious Defrauding of the +65Land. Unable to witness it any longer, I went away, sighing deeply.

7 THE UNLIMITED POWER OF PRINCES AND THE STRATAGEMS OF THEIR OFFICIALS. "The best is yet to come, " Searchall remarked, "come and see the rule of kings, princes, and other rulers who reign over their subjects by hereditary right; perhaps, you will be pleased with that." We then entered a room where we saw men sitting on such lofty and broad seats that but few could approach or reach them otherwise save by means of mechanical contrivance. Each of these men had long tubes placed in his ears, into which those wishing to communicate with him were obliged to speak. But the tubes were so twisted and full of holes that many words were lost before they reached the ruler's ear. Morevover, the words which did reach his ear were for the greatest part distorted. For that reason I noticed that the petitioners did not always receive an answer; for even though some of them cried loudly, they were not able to reach the ruler's mind. Sometimes one received an answer, but it was irrelevant to the question. The rulers likewise used tubes instead of their eyes and tongue, through which things appeared otherwise than they really were; the answers likewise differed from those intended by the rulers. Perceiving this, I remarked: "But why do they not lay aside those tubes and simply use their own eyes, ears, and tongue just like other folk?" "On account of the dignity of their person and the honor of their position, " my interpreter answered. "Do you consider them peasants that they should permit everyone to rub against their eyes, ears, and tongue?"

8 HOW INCONVENIENT IS THE NECESSITY OF HAVING COUNSELLORS. Just then I perceived certain individuals about the thrones, some of whom, disregarding the tubes, blew some vapors into the rulers' ears, others placed glasses of one or another color on his nose, or burned incense under his nose, or manipulated his hands, or directed his feet, binding or loosening them; while some strengthened and stabilized the seat under them. Observing all this, I inquired: "Who are these persons and what are they doing?" "They are privy counsellors, keeping the king and the great lords informed, " my interpreter answered. "Were I in the place of these great lords, I would not tolerate these people about me but would insist upon the freedom of my limbs and actions. " "A single individual should not depend upon himself so entirely, nor is it permitted them to do so, " he answered. "Then these great lords are worse off than peasants, for they are so bound that without the consent of others they may not even move. " "But on the other hand, " he continued, "they are thus more certain of themselves. Look at these!"

  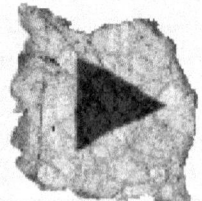

CHAPTER XX

THE MILITARY CALLING

CRUELTY OF MAN. We then entered the last street, in the very first square of which we saw a mob of men dressed in red. I approached them and overheard them discussing how to give wings to death so that it could transport itself instantly from a great distance as well as from nearby. They also debated how to destroy in an hour what had required many years to build. I was terrified by such talk, for all that I had hitherto heard and observed of human labors concerned devising and executing plans for the upbuidling and multiplying of the human race and for the comforts of human life. But these men were discussing how to destroy human life and comfort. "They really have the same aims as the rest, " my interpreter remarked, "but their methods are slightly different. They work by clearing away the obstacles. You will understand it later."

2 RECRUITING. We then approached the gate where we saw, instead of gate-keepers, a number of drummers who asked all who desired to enter for their purses. When each produced and opened it, they filled it with money and said: "This skin is paid for."

3 THE ARSENAL OR ARMORY. Thereupon they took the recruit into a cellar from which he emerged encasedd in iron and fire. Then they ordered him to proceed to the square. Desiring to see what was in the cellar, I descended into it. There I beheld heaps of weapons lying on the ground, piled up in enormous stacks and covering all the walls as far as the eye could see, so that many thousands of wagon loads would not suffice to remove the accumulation. There were all kinds of terrible weapons for piercing, hacking, slashing, stabbing, felling, chopping, severing, tearing, burning, and, in a word, killing: they mere made of iron, lead, wood, and stone. "What wild beasts are these weapons intended for?" I cried out, seized with terror. "Against men, " rejoined my interpreter. "Against men?" I echoed. "I though they were against some mad beasts or wild, ferocious animals. But, in God's name, what a cruelty for men to invent such frightful weapons against men?" "Are you so pampered?" he answered, laughing at me.

4 THE LIFE OF SOLDIERS IS LICENTIOUS. Coming out, we proceeded farther into the square where I saw those iron-clad swash-bucklers, equipped with horns and claws, bound one to another in herds. They were just lying down in front of troughs and jugs into which their food and drink had been dumped and poured, and which they gobbled and lapped, vying with each other in haste. "Are they swine fattening for the slaughter-house?" I remarked; "I indeed perceive human appearance, but swinish behavior." "Such is the privilege of this particular calling, " replied my interpreter. Just then they got up from the troughs and began dancing, skipping, frolicking, and shouting. "Observe now the delights of their life," my interpreter continued. "What do they worry about! Is it not merry here?" "I shall wait for what follows, " I replied. In the meantime, the soldiers began chasing and robbing the civilians whom they chanced to encounter. Then casting themselves on the ground, they committed all kinds of sodomy and lechery without the slightest trace of shame or fear of God until I blushed. "This should not be tolerated!" I exclaimed. "But it must be tolerated, " rejoined my interpreter, "for their calling demands every kind of freedom." Thereupon they sat down and again began gorging themselves until, surfeited to dumbness with eating and drinking, they flopped down and fell to snoring. Then they were led out to the square and there exposed to rain, snow, hail, frost, sleet, thirst, hunger and other discomforts; hence not a few of them shook, trembled, pined away, and perished, to become food for dogs and crows. But the rest took no heed of them, continuing their revels.

5 DESCRIPTION OF THE BATTLE. Suddenly drums sounded, trumpets blared, and a tumultuous crying arose. The soldiers jumped up and seizing their daggers, dirks, poniards, or whatever else each had, began to plunge them mercilessly into each other until blood spurted all around. They cut and hacked each other worse than the most ferocious beasts. The din increased in all directions; one heard the beat of horses' hoofs, the clanging of cuirasses, the clash of swords, the booming of cannon, the whizzing of shots and bullets past the ear, the blare of trumpets, the beating of drums, the outcries of those urging on the battle, the shouts of the victors, the shrieks of the wounded and the dying. In one place I saw a terrible hail of lead; in another I saw the frightful lightning of fire and heard the sound of thundering. Here a soldier lost his arm, the head, or a leg; in another, I saw the frightful lightning of fire and heard the sound of thundering. Here a soldier lost his arm, the head, or a leg; there they fell one upon the other in a heap, all writhing in pools of +67blood. "Almighty God, what is happening?" I cried out; "is the world collapsing?" Gathering my wits somewhat, I ran away from that place scarcely knowing how and whither; then stopping to catch my breath, but still trembling all over, I cried reproachfully to my guides: "What pandemonium have you led me into?" "Is there a greater mollycoddle than you?" my interpreter retorted. "To be able to attack others is to be a man!" "But what wrong have they done each other?" I persisted. "Their masters disagreed and it had to be settled in this manner, " he replied. "Oh, is this a mere settling of a disagreement?" I exclaimed. "Why, of course!" he rejoined. "For how could the disagreements of great lords, kings, and kingdoms, which acknowledge no judge over them, otherwise be settled? They must determine such cases among themselves by the sword. Whoever flourishes his sword and directs his fire more dexterously, his contention wins the day." "Oh, the barbarity and the beastliness of it!" I cried, "are there no other ways of +68pacification? Such methods of peacemaking befit wildbeasts, not men!"

6 SURVIVORS OF THE BATTLE. Just then I perceived not a few with severed arms, or legs, or a split skull or nose, with riddled bodies, or lacerated skin, all bespattered with blood, being led or carried from the battlefield. I could hardly bear to look upon them for pity. "It will all heal; a soldier must be hardy, " my interpreter remarked. "But what about those who had lost their lives altogether?" I asked. "Their skin had already been paid for," he rejoined. "How is that?" I inquired. "Didn't you notice the comforts they had been granted?" "Yes, but I likewise observed how much discomfort they had to suffer, " I replied. "But even if they have previously lived in the utmost pleasure, it is a miserable thing to feed a man in order straightway to lead him to a slaughter-house. This is a disgusting career, taken all in all; and I will have nothing to do with it. Let us go away."

CHAPTER XXI

THE KNIGHTLY ORDER

WHEREFORE NOBILITY AND COATS-OF-ARMS ARE BESTOWED. "Observe at least how highly honored are those who fight valiantly and win against all swords, pikes, arrows, and bullets, " my interpreter said. Thereupon, they led me to a palace where I saw a personage sitting under a majestic canopy, summoning before him such as had proved themselves valorous. Many came, bringing their enemies' skulls, limbs, ribs, and hands, as well as pillaged and plundered purses and bags; receiving in return his praise for these deeds, and the personage under the canopy presented them with a painted device, granting them certain extraordinary privileges above those enjoyed by all others; which they stuck on a staff and carried about for the admiration of all.

2 OTHERS ALSO CROWD INTO THIS CLASS. Observing this, others followed suit; for not only those of the fighting class, as had been the custom formerly, but many from the artisan and the learned classes presented themselves, although boasting neither scars nor plunder taken from their enemies; instead, they presented their purses or their scribblin made into books. Thereupon, they received the same rewards as the others, although their devices were commonly even more splendid, and were admitted to an upper hall.

3 POMP OF KNIGHT. I followed them and saw groups of them promenading with plumed bonnets, spurred heels, and steel at their sides. I dared not approach close to them, and it was well that I did not. For I soon observed how ill it fared those who dared mix with them. Some wretches who had but brushed against their side, or had not made enough room for them quickly enough, or had not bowed low enough, or had not pronounced their titles clearly enough, met with blows. Fearing a similar maltreatment, I begged that we go away. "First examine them a little better. But be careful!" Mr. Searchall insisted.

4 KNIGHTLY DEEDS. Thereupon, I observed their actions from a distance; I found that their work (according to the privileges of their order, as they said) consisted of pounding the pavement up and down, of hanging their legs astride a horse; chasing greyhounds, hares, and wolves; driving serfs to hard labor; clapping them into dungeons and freeing them again; stretching their legs as long as possible under their tables loaded with a variety of dishes; bowing to ladies and kissing their fingers; playing professionally at draughts and dice, of telling shamefully smutty and obscene stories; and the like. It was, so they said, certified in their privileges that whatever they do must be esteemed noble, and that no one but an honorable person might associate with them. Some measured and compared their shields with one another; the more ancient and dilapidated the shield, the greater honor it was accorded; those carrying a new shield were regarded by the rest with derisive head-shaking. I saw many other things there which appeared queer and absurd; but I must not speak of them all. This only shall I add, that having sufficiently scanned all these puerilities, I again implored my guides to depart, and my wish was granted.

5 THE ROAD TO THE CASTLE OF FORTUNE. As we went along, my interpreter remarked: "Well, you have already investigated the labors and occupations of mankind and yet liked none; perhaps it is because you think that these people have nothing but ceaseless toil. Nevertheless you must realize that all their labor is merely the means to the attainment of leisure which all who have not spared themselves finally obtain; that when they gain wealth, possessions, fame, honors, comfort, and pleasure, their mind has plenty in which to delight. Let us, therefore, lead you to the Castle of Delight that you may see the goal of all human labors." Thereat I rejoiced, promising myself rest and solace for my mind.

CHAPTER XXII

THE PILGRIM FINDS HIMSELF AMONG THE NEWSMONGERS

NEWSMONGERS ARE AMAZED BY MANY THINGS. Approaching the gate, I caught sight to the left of the square of a large group of people. "Why, we must not pass these men unnoticed!" Mr. Ubiquitous exclaimed. "What are they doing?" I inquired. "Come and see!" he rejoined. We mingled with them and they, standing by twos or threes, gesticulated with their fingers, or shook their heads, or clapped their hands, or scratched themselves behind their ears. Finally some of them cried aloud for joy, while others burst out weeping. "What is going on here?" I inquired; "are they acting a comedy?" "No, indeed!" replied my interpreter; do not mistake this for a play. They are dealing with real matters, at which they amazed, amused, or angered, as the case may be." "I should like to know, " said I, "what amazes, amuses, or angers them." Then I perceived that they had some whistles, and leaning close to one another's ear, they blew them: when the sound was pleasant, they were glad; when it was shrill, they were troubled.

2 WHISTLES HAVE DIVERS SOUNDS. But one thing particularly puzzled me: the sound of the identical whistle gladdened some so greatly that they could not refrain from dancing for joy, while it so pained others that they stopped up their ears and ran away; or listening to it, burst out into lamentations and bitter tears. "Is not it odd that the same whistle should sound so sweetly to some and so sourly to others?" I said. "The difference is not in sound but in hearing, " my interpreter answered. "For as patients are affected differently by the same, according to their disease, so in this case. It depends on the inner disposition and inclination to the thing how one is affected by the external sound, whether sweet or bitter."

3 THE LIMPING MESSENGER. "But where do they get those whistles?" I inquired. "They are brought from everywhere, " he answered; "do you not see the dealers?" So I looked about and behold! persons walking or riding who were specially appointed to distribute the whistles. Many rode swift horses, and there were many people who bought from them; others walked on foot, or hopped on crutches: and the wise folk bought from these men, saying that their goods were more reliable.

4 THE DELIGHT OF NEWS. Not only did I watch them, but I even stopped occasionally to listen to them; and felt a certain pleasure in hearing so many different voices coming from all directions. But what displeased me was the fact that some were immoderately given to the practice of buying all the whistles they could get, and after blowing each in turn a while, of throwing them away. Moreover, there were men of different classes who seldom stayed home, but were constantly watching in the square, keeping their ears open, not to miss the faintest whistle.

5 VANITY OF NEWSMONGERING. I became very displeased with the business when I perceived the futility of it. For often a sad sound was given out, and all grew mournful; but shortly thereatter another sound came, and the fright was turned into laughter. Again, the sound of a particular whistle was so pleasant that all were filled with delight and joy; but suddenly it ceased or was changed into a shrill noise: hence those who had given credence to it were disappointed as having hoped or feared in vain, since all went up in smoke. It was, consequently, amusing to see that they were people so light-minded as to allow themselves to be duped by every gust of wind. Therefore I praised those who paid no attention to these follies but attended to their own business.

6 DISCOMFORT BOTH FROM NEWS AND WITHOUT IT. But then I perceievd another disadvantage: namely, that when some paid no attention to what was being whistld, they sometimes came to grief on that account. Finally, I observed that the handling of those whistles was dangerous in many ways. For since the sounds affected different ears differently, quarrels and fights often resulted as happened to me. For having come upon a particularly fine and clear-sounding whistle, I passed it on to my friend; but others, snatching it away, threw it on the ground and stamped upon it, scolding me for spreading gossip; seeing them so heated in their anger, I was obliged to run away. Meanwhile, as my guides were cheering me with promises of the Castle of Fortune, we proceeded thither.

CHAPTER XXIII

THE PILGRIM INVESTIGATES THE CASTLE OF FORTUNE

VIRTUE, A FORGOTTEN GATE TO FAME. Arriving before that fine castle, I caught sight, first of all, of a large crowd of people gathered there from all the streets of the city, walking around it and seeking entrance into it. There was but a single steep and narrow gate leading into the castle; but it was in ruins, having been choked with debris and overgrown with thorns; it was called, I think, Virtue. I was told that in former times this had been built as the only means of access to the castle, but that it had been ruined soon afterwards in some accident; thereupon, many smaller gates were made and the original gate was abandoned on account of its steepness, inaccessibility, and difficulty of entrance.

2 SIDE-ENTRANCES. The walls, then, having been broken through, several smaller gates had been built from both sides; I scanned the names inscribed over them: Hypocrisy, Lie, Flattery, Unrighteousness, Cunning, Force, and so forth, but while I was reading them aloud, those who were entering the gates heard me and were incensed with anger against me and threatened to throw me down the hill; I was, therefore, forced to be silent. I also perceived that a few were still clambering up through the debris and the thorns to the old gate, but only a few of them were able to get through, while the rest failed; these latter returned and went to the lower gates and entered through them.

3 FORTUNE PROMOTES THOSE WHOM SHE SEIZES BY CHANCE. Having also entered, I saw that this was not the castle proper but only its forecourt, in which were multitudes of people, wistfully looking up to the higher palaces and sighing. When I inquired what they were doing, I was informed that they were awaiting a glance from the gracious Dame Fortune in order to be admitted into the castle. "But will not all these people in the end gain admittance?" I asked, "they all have toiled faithfully for that purpose." "It is up to each one to exert himself as much as he knows how or is able to, " my guide answered; "in the end, however, it rests with Dame Fortune whether or not she wishes to admit him. You may observe for yourself how it works. " I then noticed that there were neither steps nor gates leading higher up but only a large wheel perpetually in motion. By grasping it, a man could be lifted to the floor above, where he would then be received by Dame Fortune and allowed to proceed further. However, not every one below was able to grasp the wheel, but only such as had been led to it or had been placed upon it by an official of Dame Fortune, Chance by name: it slipped out of the grasp of all the rest. This regent, Chance, walked among the crowd, selecting people in a haphazard fashion and seating them on the wheel: but although others pressed themselves into her view or stretched their hands toward her and begged her, pleading their past toil, sweat, callouses, scars, or other deserts, it was all in vain. I hold that she must have been totally deaf and blind, for she neither looked at anyone nor heeded his pleading.

4 THE SAD CASE OF THOSE WHO SEEK FORTUNE. Many people of various classes entered by means of their profession through the gate of Virtue or through the side-gates; as I had observed them previously, they had spared no toil or trouble, but awaited happiness in vain; yet another, who perhaps had not been even thinking about the matter, was taken by the hand and lifted up. Many of these who waited were filled with utter despondency that their turn would not come, so that now a few of them grew grey in the meantime; many in despair gave up all hope of happiness and returned to their drudgery; but some were again seized with longing and returned to the castle, pushing themselves before the eyes and within the reach of Dame +69Fortune; thus I observed that in either case the state of these people as wretched and miserable.

CHAPTER XXIV

THE PILGRIM EXAMINES THE LIFE OF THE RICH

Thereupon, I said to my guide: "I should like to examine the upper palace and observe the honors accorded by Dame Fortune to her guests." "Very well," said he, and before I realized it, he lifted me up along with himself; there I saw Dame Fortune standing on a sphere, distributing crowns, scepters, ruling offices, chains, decorations, purses, titles, honors, honey, and other delights, and the recipients were permitted to proceed above. Scanning the plan of the castle, I noticed that it consisted of three stories and observed that some of the people were taken to the lower, some to the middle, and the rest to the upper rooms. My interpreter explained: "Here in the lower story dwell those who are honored by Dame Fortune with money and wealth; in the middle rooms are those whom she regales with dainties; while the upper palace is occupied by those who are decked in glory, to be seen, praised, and honored by the rest. Some are favored with two or even all three kinds of gifts; and these may go wherever they please. You see what a happy thing it is to gain admittance to this place!"

2 THE FETTERS AND BURDENS OF WEALTH. "Let us go first of all among those on this floor, then," I said. We entered the lower chambers, but found them dark and gloomy, so that at first I could hardly distinguish anything, but only heard a jingling sound. And I was assailed from all corners by a fetid smell. When my eyes became accustomed to the darkness a little, I perceived men of all classes, walking, standing, sitting, or lying, all with their feet bound in fetters and their hands in chains; some of them had a chain even around their necks and a burden on their backs. I stood horror-stricken and cried out: "What, for goodness' sake, have we entered a prison?" "How silly you are!" my interpreter replied, laughing. "Why, these are the gifts of Dame Fortune which she has bestowed upon her dear sons." I examined those gifts of one, then another, and a third, but found them fetters of steel, chains of iron, and wicker-baskets full of lead or soil. "What strange gifts!" I exclaimed; "I am sure I would not care for any of them." "You fool, you look at these things wrongly," my interpreter retorted; "they are all pure gold!" I looked again and scrutinized them more closely, but reaffirmed that I could see nothing but iron and soil. "Well, then, do not be such a sophist," he replied, "and believe others rather than yourself; see how they value their possessions!"

3 I looked about and saw a wonder; for those poor wretches took the greatest delight in their bondage. One counted the links of his chain, another took them apart and reassembled them, or weighed the chain in his hand, or measured it by the span, or lifted it to his lips and kissed it, or sought to protect it against frost, heat, or injury by wrapping it in a kerchief. Here and there groups of two or three came together to compare their chains by measuring and weighing them in their hands; he whose chain was lighter was grieved and envied his neighbors, while the possessor of the larger or heavier chain strutted about arrogantly, priding himself and boasting. But there were others who, sitting quietly in obscure corners, secretly delighted in the size of their chains and fetters, not wishing others to see them; for, I presume, they feared envy and theft. Others had coffers full of lumps of earth and stones which they constantly rearranged, shutting and opening the lids, and neither wishing nor seeking to go anywhere for fear of losing their treasures. Some did not trust even the coffers and bound and tied so many of those things upon their persons that they could neither walk nor stand, but were obliged to lie, panting and groaning. Observing this, I remarked: "But, in the name of all the saints, are these people to be considered happy? Why, among all the human toil and drudgery which I have observed below, I found nothing so miserable as this happiness!" "It is indeed true (why should we deny it?)" Mr. Searchall answered, "that the mere possession of these gifts of Fortune without the use of them is greater trouble than delight." "Nevertheless it is not Dame Fortune's fault," interposed my interpreter, "that some people do not know how to use her gifts. She is not stingy with them, but some of these churlish misers do not know how to turn them either to their own or anybody else's comfort. Nevertheless, after all, say what you will, it is a great happiness to possess wealth." "I care nothing for such happiness as I see here," I replied.

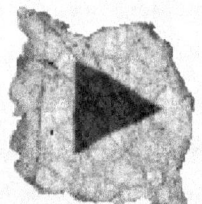

CHAPTER XXV

THE LIFE OF THE VOLUPTUARIES

MULIEBRAL VOLUPTUARIES. "Let us go upstairs and there you shall find nothing but genuine pleasures, I promise you, " Mr. Searchall remarked. So we went upstairs an entered the first hall; I beheld several rows of suspended and swinging couches piled high with downy feather-beds: the people lolling on them were surrounded by swarms of servants with fly-swatters and fans and other contrivances in their hands, ever ready for all manner of service. Whenever one of them wished to arise, hands from all sides were instantly stretched out to him; dressing, he was offered nothing but the softest silk garments; whenever he wished to go anywhere, he was carried on litters upholstered with cushions. "Behold, here you have the comfort you have been seeking!" exclaimed my interpreter, "what more could you ask? To possess such abundance of every good thing so as to have no need of taking thought for anything, to be spared the touch of all toil, to have everything one's soul desires, to allow no ill wind to blow on you, is not this a blessed state?" "These halls certainly are more cheerful than those torture chambers beneath, " I answered, "but even here I do not find everything to my liking. " "What is amiss again?" he asked. "I dislike these lazy fellows with bulging eyes, bloated faces, swollen bellies, and untouchable limbs which hurt like an inflamed boil," I replied, "if they touch anything or anyone brushes against them, or if they are caught in a draft, they straightway sicken. Stagnant water rots and stinks, I have heard, and here I see examples of it. These men do not enjoy life because they sleep it away and waste it; there is nothing here to attract me." "What a queer philosopher you are!" remarked my interpreter.

2 GAMES AND PLAYS. Then they led me into another hall where my eyes and ears were greeted with new charms: I saw delightful gardens, pools, and game preserves, with game, birds, an fish; the air was filled with charming music; I also saw jolly crowds, frolicking, chasing one another, dancing, pursuing each other, fencing, playing games, and I know not what else. "This is no stagnant water, " remarked my interpreter. "That is true, " I replied; "but permit me to investigate closer." After observing them, I remarked: "I notice that none of these folk eats and drinks his fill of those frolics; but getting tired of them and runs to seek other amusements. This appears but a trivial delight to me." "If you look for delights in eating and drinking, " he said, "let us step into this hall."

THE GLUTTONS. We then entered a third hall; here I saw men seated at tables and boards loaded with everything in abundance; feasting merrily. I approached and observed how some gorged themselves continually with food and drink so that their bellies could scarcely contain it all and they were obliged to let out their belts; some were so glutted that the food spilld up and down. Others chose only the daintiest bits, and smacking their lips, wished they had crane's necks (in order to enjoy the taste longer). Some boasted that for ten or twenty years they had never seen a sunrise or sunset: for at sunset they were already drunk and at sunrise they were not yet sober. Neither did they sit in gloomy silence, but had to be entertained with music to which each joined his voice, so that the noises one heard were as if made by various beasts and birds; one howled, another roared, or crowed, barked, whistled, chirped, or twittered, accompanying their performance with grotesque gestures.

4 THE PILGRIM'S FEAST AMONG THE GOURMANDS. Thereupon my interpreter asked me how I liked the harmony. "Not a bit," I replied. "Will you ever find anything to your liking?" he retorted, "are you a stump that even this merriment cannot enliven you?" Then several gourmands from behind the tables caught sight of me and one began to drink my health: another winked at me, inviting me to sit down with him; a third began to question me as to who I was and what was my business there, while a fourth demanded rudely why I did not wish them a "God bless you!" I was incensed and cried out: "You dare to ask God's blessing on such swinish gluttony?" Before I had quite uttered those words, however, there rained upon me such a hailstorm of plates, platters, cups, and glasses that I hardly had time to dodge them, and gathering myself, to rush out. But, after all, it was easier for me, a sober man, to flee than for those drunken sots to hit me. "See, did I not tell you long ago to hold your tongue and stop scolding? Try to adjust yourself to others instead of imagining that they must follow the conceits of your shallow pate."

HE WENT BACK AGAIN. Mr. Ubiquitous burst out laughing, and taking me by the hand, said: "Let us go back again." Nevertheless, I refused. He urged me: "There is still much for you to observe, which you could have seen, had you held your tongue. Now let us return; but be careful; it were better to stand at a distance." I allowed myself to be persuaded and entered again. And why should I deny it? I was persuaded to sit down at a table and to permit toasts be drunk in my honor, and drained my own cups to the bottom, desiring to discover at last what enjoyment there was in it. I even joined in the singing, shouting, and frolicking: in short, I behaved like the rest. Nevertheless, I did so somewhat timidly, for it appeared to me quite unbecoming. When others saw my clumsy attempts, they laughed at me, while some stormed at me for not draining my cups fast enough. In the meantime, something began to gnaw under my coat and to thump under my cap, and to force itself out of my throat; my legs began to stagger; my tongue to stammer and my head to swim, and I began to feel angry with myself and with my leaders and openly to declare that this was crass bestiality not worthy of human beings; particularly after I scrutinized the delights of these voluptuaries still more closely.

6 THE WRETCHED WAY OF VOLUPTUARIES. For I heard some complain that they had no appetite for food or drink, nor could they force it down their throats any more; others, pitying them, and in order to help them, ordered merchants to scour and search the world for such foodstuffs as would prove palatable to the gourmands; cooks were bidden to use all their ingenuity in imparting to the delicacies a special fragrance, color, or taste in order to allure them into the stomachs; physicians had to resort to emetics and clysters to induce free movement of the bowels, so that one meal might make room for the other. Hence, it cost enormous amounts of toil and treasure to gather the things which they would cram and pour into their throats; much cleverness and ingenuity to convey them there; and in the end it caused them either excruciating pains and gnawing in their bellies, or it was thrown up. Furthermore, as a rule they suffered with bad tastes in the mouth, hiccoughing, burning of the stomach, and belching; they slept badly and suffered from coughing and sniffing, slobbering and running of the nose; their table and all corners were full of vomit and excrement. Walking or lying down, they suffered with putrid bellies, gouty legs, trembling hands, festering eyes, and so forth. "Are these the supposed delights?" I exclaimed, "oh, let us go away that I may not be tempted to say more and bring upon myself some rough handling again." Then averting my eyes and holding my nose, I went out.

VENERIS REGNUM. We entered another hall of the same suite of rooms where I saw multitudes of people of both sexes walking about hand in hand, embracing and kissing each other; not to mention what else.

LIBIDINIS AESTUS. Of all I saw, however, this only shall I mention as a warning to myself: all these people, locked here by Dame Fortune, were suffering with a burning, scabby skin disease which caused them perpetual itching, so that they had not respite, but wherever they went, scratched and rubbed themselves against whatever they found, until they drew blood; nevertheless, even this scratching could not relieve the itch which only grew more intense; they were indeed ashamed of it, but secretly and of out sight they did nothing but scratch themselves.

MORBUS GALLICUS. Evidently this was a most annoying and incurable disease. Besides, in not a few cases the disease broke out externally, so that they loathed each other, being repugnant and repulsive to one another; for wholesom eyes and mind it was unbearable to look on them or to endure the stench which they emitted.

LIBIDO DESPERATIONIS PRACTIUM. Finally, I observed that this room was the last of the Palace of Delights, from which one could go neither forward nor back, except that in the rear I noticed a hole through which those who had surrendered themselves completely to this lechery fell through alive and found themselves in the outer darkness surrounding the world.

CHAPTER XXVI

THE LIFE OF THE EXALTED OF THE WORLD

DISCOMFORTS OF THE EXALTED. We then ascended to the uppermost palace, which was open to the sky, having no other ceiling. There we beheld a great number of seats, some higher than others, all placed along the edges so that they could be seen from the city below, persons being seated as Dame Fortune had assigned them higher or lower places, and passersby rendered them honor (although only to their faces) by bending their knees or inclining their heads. "Behold, is it not a fine thing to be so exalted that you can be seen from all directions, so that all must look up to you?" my interpreter exclaimed. "And to be exposed so that rain, snow, and hail, heat, and cold can beat on you!" I added. "But what of it?" he retorted, "it is nevertheless a fine thing to occupy such a position that all must take notice of you and regard you." "It is true that they are regarded, " I replied, "but this regard is a greater burden than it is an honor. For each one is spied upon by so many, as I observe, that he is hardly allowed to move a finger without its being seen and criticized; what kind of comfort is that?" I was particularly confirmed in this opinion when I perceived how respectfully they were treated to their faces, while behind their backs and on their sides disrespect was heaped upon them. For behind every one of those lolling in their seats stood some who cast malignant glances at him, grimaced and contemptuously wagged their heads at thim, mocked him, and with their spittle, mucus, or something else fouled his back. Some even plotted an overthrow of the occupants, and jerked the seat from under them, and not a few of the latter met with a fall or other mishap in my presence.

2 PERILS OF THE EXALTED. For, as I have said, the seats were placed near the edge and it needed but a slight push to tip them over; thereupon, he who but a little while before had been puffed up with pride, found himself sprawling on the ground. It seemed that the seats were poised upon some such contrivance that the slightest touch instantly overturned them and he who sat on it foiund himself on the ground; the higher the seat, the easier it was to tip and to fall out of it. I also witnessed great jealousy and envious looks among the occupants; they thrust one another from the seats, usurped each other's rule, knocked down one another's crowns, and deprived each other of their titles; thus everything was in constant change; one was climbing into a seat, another was stepping down, or falling headlong from it. Observing this, I remarked: "It is hard that after the long and arduous toile which they endured before gaining their places, their reward should be of such brief duration, some hardly having begun to enjoy the glory before coming to their end." "Dame Fortune finds it necessary to distribute her honors in this fashion in order that all whom she desires to honor may share in them, " my interpreter answered. "One must give place to another."

CHAPTER XXVII

THE GLORY OF THE FAMOUS IN THE WORLD

Moreover, those who behave well here," continued my interpreter, "or otherwise deserve it, are honored by Dame Fortune in still another fashion, namely, by immortality." "Really?" I exclaimed; "that is indeed a glorious thing, to be made immortal. Show me how." Thereupon, Mr. Searchall turned me around and pointed out to me a still higher place or eminence on the western side of the palace, also under the open sky and accessible by means of steps, at the foot of which was a small door, at which sat a man (called a Censor vulgi, Mr. Judgeall), who had, grotesquely enough, eyes and ears all over his body, and everyone desiring entrance to the Hall of Fame was obliged not only to report to him, but likewise to produce and deliver for his verdict all those claims by which he deemed himself worthy of immortality. If his deeds comprised anything remarkable or extraordinary, whether good or bad, he was permitted to go up; if not, he was left below. Most of those who were admitted, as I observed, were members of the governing, military, and the learned classes; while the religious, the artisan, and the domestic classes were represented by a smaller number.

2 GLORY IS GRANTED EVEN IF UNMERITED. I was much irritated to observe that as many wicked men (such as robbers, tyrants, adulterers, murderers, and incendiaries) were granted admittance as good persons. For I felt that this could but result in the encouragement of the perverse in their vices; thus, for instance, one came requesting immortality, and when asked what deed worthy of immortal memory he had done, he answered that he had purposely destroyed the most famous object in the world he knew, a temple which had been constructed by the toil and treasure of seventeen kingdoms during a period of three hundred years. He had burned it down and had reduced it to ruins in a single day. Even the Censor was astonished at such shameful vandalism and at first refused him admittance, deeming him unworthy. But Dame Fortune came and ordered that he be admitted. This example encouraged others who came and expatiated upon the many horrible crimes which they had committed; one that he had shed so much human blood as he could; another, that he had invented a new blasphemy wherewith to revile God; another, that he had sentenced God to death; another, that he had pulled the sun from the sky and had plunged it into an abyss; another that he had organized a new band of incendiaries and murderers for the purging of the human race, and all these were forthwith admitted to the upper hall; this as I have said displeased me greatly.

3 VANITY OF FAME. I passed through the door after these people and beheld there another official of Dame Fortune, Fame by name, who received the would-be immortals. She consisted entirely of mouths. As the official below was full of eyes and ears, this one was entirely covered with mouths and tongues from which issued not a little noise and sound, the benefit derived therefrom by the precious candidates for immortality consisted in having their names, by means of Fame's cries, made known far and wide. But when I investigated the matter closely, I perceived that the clamor made about each new arrival gradually subsided until it died down altogether, and somebody else's name was taken up. "What kind of immortality is this," I remonstrated, "when each man's glory persists only momentarily in the eyes, mouths, and minds of humankind, and then ceases altogether?" "Nothing seems to be enough for you," my interpreter replied, "at least, look at these, then!"

4 IS IT NOT FUTILE TO ENTER INTO HISTORY?

3 VANITY OF FAME. I turned around and perceived that some painters, sitting and looking at a few of these men, were painting their portraits. I inquired why they were doing so. My interpreter explained: "This is done in order that their memory may not wane and cease as the sound of the voice does; the memory of these men will endure forever." I looked and behold! All these people who had their portraits painted were thrown out into the abyss just like all the rest; only their portrait remained behind. Thereupon, these pictures were hoisted upon a staff, so that they could be seen by all. "What sort of immortality is this," I expostulated again; "for in truth nothing but the paper and the paint bearing the name of their likeness remains, while they themselves perish as miserably as the rest! This is deceit, by God, nothing but deceit! What do I care whether somebody has daubed my likeness on a piece of paper when in the meantime who knows what has become of me? I care nothing for it!" Hearing this, my interpreter roundly scolded me for being a crack-brained idiot and insisted that a man of such generally contrary notions had no place in the world.

5 MUCH FALSEHOOD IN HISTORY. Thereupon, I relapsed into silence. Then I espied another falsehood. The portrait of one, whom I had known in life to have been handsome and splendid, was most hideous; while another, who had been ugly, was as beautiful as the painters could make him; of some, they painted two, three, or four portraits, each different; so that I was angered partly at the carelessness and partly at the lack of fidelity of the painters. Moreover, I became aware of the futility of this. For examining these pictures, I found many of them black with age, dusty, decaying or rotting, so that very little or nothing at all could be discerned in them; there were such heaps of them that one could not be seen for another, so that they

were scarcely ever examined by anyone; such, then, was glory!

6 ERECTED MEMORIALS ALSO PERISH. Meanwhile, Dame Fortune would come and order not only old and decayed, but even new portraits to be thrown out; I realized that this precious immortality was not only of no intrinsic worth, but also depended entirely upon the senseless whim of Dame Fortune (who either admitted the portraits to her castle or ordered them thrown out); and beyond that there was nothing of which one could be certain; this made her and her gifts so much the more odious to me. For she treated all her sons, as she walked about the castle, in the same manner, augmenting or diminshing the pleasures of the voluptuaries or the wealth of the rich, but likewise suddenly taking it all away from them and turning them out of doors.

7 DEATH AT LAST ANNIHILATES ALL. Likewise Death, which I noticed appearing at the castle and removing them one by one, although not all in the same manner, increased my terrors. The rich she brought down either by her ordinary arrows, or, kneeling, she strangled and suffocated them with their chains; the voluptuaries she dispatched by mixing poisons with their dainties; the famous she hurled down from their seats and broke their necks or dispatched them with rapiers, muskets, or daggers, almost every one of them being sent out of the world in some such violent manner.

  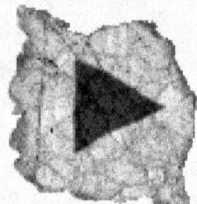

CHAPTER XXVIII

THE PILGRIM BEGINS TO DESPAIR AND QUARRELS WITH HIS LEADERS

SAPIENTIAE APEX, DESPERATIO DE REBUS MUNDI*. I began to fear that the true satisfaction, in which alone my mind could feel wholly secure and certain, was to be found neither in the world nor even in the castle itself. These thoughts oppressed me more and more sorely; nor could my interpreter, Mr.Delusion (despite all his efforts) bring me relief. Finally I cried out: "Oh, woe is me! Shall I ever find satisfaction in this miserable world? For all things are full of futility and misery!" "Whose fault is it, you spoilsport, but your own?" my interpreter retorted, "for you detest everything which should please you! Look at others who gay and well content they are in their callings, having found sufficient sweetness in their own lot!" "They are either insane altogether, " I expostulated with him, "or they lie; for it is not possible that they should enjoy true happiness." "Then become insane like them, " retorted Ubiquitous, "if it will ease your sorrow." "I am not able to manage even that, as you yourself well know, " I replied. "For how many times have I tried it, but perceiving the violent changes and the miserable end of it all, I gave it up."

2 THE MIND OF MAN DOES NOT FIND IN THE WORLD WHAT IT SEEKS "What else causes it but your own fantasies?" rejoined my interpreter. "Were you not so fastidious about all human affairs and did you not toss them about like a swine does a straw-wisp, you would possess, like all the rest, a peaceful mind and enjoy pleasure, joy, and happiness." "That is to say, " I answered, "if I, like you, accepted the external appearance of things, and took some stale witticism for joy, the perusal of some literary hodgepodge for wisdom, and a bit of accidental fortune for the apex of satiety! But what of the sweat, the tears, aches, confusion, short-comings, accidents, and all the other misfortunes without number, extent, and limit among all classes? Alas! alas the sorrow of this miserable life! You have led me through everything, and to what avail? You have promised and exhibited to me wealth, knowledge, comfort, and security. But which of these do I possess? None. What have I learned? Nothing. Where am I? I myself know not. This only I know, that after so much danger, and after exhausting and wearying of my mind I find nothing in the end by an inward pain in myself and the hatred of others toward me.

3 "It serves you right!" my interpreter retorted, "why have you disdained my advice which has been from the beginning that you distrust nothing but believe everything; that you test nothing but accept all; that you criticize nothing but be pleased with everything? Had you taken that path, you would have traveled tranquilly and would have found favor with men and pleasure for yourself." "Having been doubtless neatly deceived by you, " I answered, "I should have raved, like the rest; wandering to and fro, I should have rejoiced; groaning under a burden, I should have frolicked; sick and dying, I should have shouted for joy. I saw, observed, and learned that neither I nor anyone else is anything, knows anything, or possesses anything, but that we all but imagine ourselves to know something. We grasp at a shadow while the truth escapes us. Woe to us!"

4 WHO SEES THROUGH THE WORLD CANNOT BUT GRIEVE. "I repeat what I said before, " my interpreter rejoined; "you yourself are to blame for your condition, because you demand something great and extraordinary, such as is granted to no one." "Consequently I grieve even more, " I replied, "that not only I myself, but the whole human race is so miserable; and so blind that it is not conscious of its own miseries." "I do not know how and by what means to satisfy your poor addled pate," my intepreter retorted, "since there is not a single thing you like, neither the world nor the people in it, neither work nor idleness, neither learning nor ignorance, I know not what to do with you and what in the world to recommend to you." Mr. Ubiquitous then suggested: "Let us take him to the Queen's castle over there in the center; he may come to his senses there."

CHAPTER XXIX

THE PILGRIM EXAMINES THE CASTLE OF THE QUEEN OF THE WORLD, WISDOM

They took me by the hand and led me to the castle, resplendent on the outside with beautiful paintings, its gate kept by sentinels so that no one but office-holders and rulers of the world be admitted. They alone, as the servants of the Queen and the executors of her commands, were free to enter and leave: others wishing to see the castle had to be satisfied with gaping at it from the outside (for it was deemed improper for everybody to spy out the secrets of the world government). Indeed I observed there a large number of gaping idlers, who made greater use of their mouths than of their eyes; I rejoiced that my guides led me to the gate, for I was eager to understand the secrets of the Wisdom of the world.

2 Even this did not pass without incident: for the sentinels barred my way and demanded what my business in the castle was; then they began to drive and push me back, threatening me with menacing gestures. But Mr. Ubiquitous, as one known to them, answered I know not what in my behalf, and taking me by the hand, led me into the first court.

3 Scanning the buildings of the castle itself, I noted its dazzling white walls which were said to be of alabaster; but when I scrutinized them more closely and touched them, I found that they consisted of nothing but paper, the cracks in which revealed the two underneath; so I judged that the walls were hollow and stuffed with tow, and was so amazed at this piece of deception that I laughed aloud. We came to the stairs leading up somewhere: but I hesitated to go up for fear of falling through (or perhaps because my heart had a premonition of what was to befall me there). My interpreter reproached me, saying: "What kind of fantasy is this, my friend? You might as well be afraid that the sky will fall on you. Do you not see the multitudes ascending and descending?" Seeing the example of others, I began to ascend the spiral staircase which was so high that one was likely to grow dizzy.

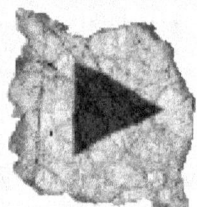

CHAPTER XXX

THE PILGRIM IS ACCUSED AT THE PALACE OF WISDOM

THE PILGRIM IS BROUGHT BEFORE THE QUEEN OF WORLDLY WISDOM. They led me into a certain spacious hall where I was at first dazzled by the extraordinary brilliance of the light that streamed not only through the many windows, but was more especially reflected from the previous stones with which (I was told) the wall were studded. The floor was covered with expensive rugs resplendent with gold; instead of a ceiling, there was something that appeared like a cloud or a mist. But I had no time to examine it carefully; for my eyes rested instantly on that precious Queen herself, sitting upon a high throne, under a canopy, and was surrounded on both sides by her advisors and attendants, a retinue of an amazingly majestic mien. I was awestruck by such splendor, especially when they began, one after another, to cast glances at me. "Fear nothing, but approach closer, " Mr. Ubiquitous whispered, "so that Her Majest the Queen may see you; be of good courage, but do not forget humility and civility." He then led me to the middle of the room and ordered me to make a low bow; which, although I did not know how to do, yet I performed somehow.

2 AND IS IMPEACHED. Then the interpreter, making himself my spokesman without my consent, began his speech as follows: "Most illustrious Queen of the world, the brightest beam of God, august Wisdom! This young man, whom we have brought before your honorable countenance, had been so fortunate as to receive permission from Fate, your Grace's regent, to travel through and to examine all the groups and orders of this most glorious kingdom of the world. The Most High has placed you in His stead as the ruler of the world, that by your providence you may rule it from one end to the other. This young man, then, has been conducted by us, who have been designated by your providence for such service, through all the classes of mankind. But (we confess it with humility and pain) despite all our sincere and faithful endeavors, we have been unable to induce him to take a liking to any occupation in which he might settle peacefully and become one of the faithful, obedient, and permanent citizens of this our common land; for he has shown himself forever displeased and has found fault with everything and has a longing for some other extraordinary thing. Being unable either to understand or to satisfy this wild desire of his, we have brought him before your august Majesty and commend him to your province to do with him as you see fit."

3 AND BECAME APPREHENSIVE. Hearing this unexpected speech, I was thrown, as anyone might well imagine, into an apprehensive state of mind. I clearly saw that I had been brought here to trial, and hence was filled with fear, particularly as I perceived a ferocious beast lying near the throne of the Queen (whether it was a dog or a lynx or some dragon, I do not well know), its shining eyes riveted upon me: I noticed that a single word would have sufficed to have it spring upon me.

THE ADVERSARY. Besides, two courtiers, the Queen's guards stood there, who were indeed dressed in women's apparel, but were, nevertheless, terrible to behold; especially the one on the left.

POWER. For this guard was clad in a suit of armor studded with sharp points like a hedgehog (so that it was dangerous even to touch him, as I perceived), having steel claws on his feet and hands and held a spear and a sword in one hand, a bow and fire in the other.

CRAFTINESS. The other guard appeared more grotesque than terrible, instead of armor he wore a great coat lined with the fox fur but turned inside out: in place of a halberd, he held a fox-tail in his right hand and rattled a branch with nuts with his left.

4 When my interpreter (or shall I say, my betrayer) finished his speech, the Queen (whose face was covered with the finest veil), spoke to me in a serious and discursive tone. "My worthy youth, I am not ill-pleased with your desire and intention to examine all things in the world (for I gladly give my permission to any of my beloved servants who wishes such a boom, and gladly render him assistance therein through these my faithful servants and serving-maids). Just the same, I dislike to hear that you are so fastidious that insteadof learning, as behooves you, a recent guest in the world, you give yourself over to sophistication. For which reason, although I could chastise you as a warning to others, yet in order to make my forbearance and goodness more commonly known rather than my strictness, I shall bear with you a little longer and allow you to dwell here at the castle, that you may be able to understand better both yourself and my rule. Value this my grace and know that not everybody is granted permission to visit these secret places, where the decrees and policies of the world are determined." Having finished speaking, she made a motion with her hand, in accordance with which sign I stepped aside, desirous to watch the further proceedings.

5 THE ROYAL COUNSELLORS. Having stepped aside, I inquired of my interpreter about the names, order, and duties of the counsellors. "Those nearest Her Majesty the Queen are her privy counsellors, " he answered, "on her right hand stand Purity, Prudence, Deliberation, Affability and Moderation; on her left hand are Truth, Zeal, Earnestness, Valor, Patience, and Constancy; these counsellors are ever near the royal throne.

6 THE FEMALE OFFICIALS OF THE QUEEN. "The women occupying the lower level are her officials and viceregents in the world. The one in the grey skirt, veiled, is the viceregent of the lower realms and is called Insdustry ; the other, in the gold-embroidered head-dress, wearing the folded ruff and crowned with the wreath, is the viceregent of the castle of blessings, and is named Dame Fortune (but I take it that you already know her). These two, together with their maid-servants, are sometimes at their respective stations, sometimes here, where they render service as well as receive orders and directions. Both of them have their under-regents: thus Dame Industry has placed Love over the matrimonial state, Diligence over the crafts and trades, Intelligence over the scholars, Piety over the clergy, Justice over the governing class, and Courage over the soldiers."

7 THE RULE OF WOMEN IN THE WORLD. Hearing these high-sounding names, and recalling the disorder I found in the world, I was tempted to make a testy remark, but did not dare; I merely thought to myself: "What a strange order prevails in this world! The ruler is a woman, her counsellors are women, the officials are women, the whole government is feminine! No wonder nobody fears it!"

8 THE BODYGUARDS. Thereupon, I inquired about the two guards, who they were and what their task was. My interpreter informed that "even Her Majesty the Queen has enemies and foes, against whom she must guard herself. The one dressed in fox furs is named Craftiness, while the other, clad in steel and fire, is called Force; where one fails to protect, the other comes to the rescue; thus the two co-operate. The dog also serves as a guard, for by his barking he warns against, and drives away any suspicious individual; his name at the court is Warner, but some who dislike his duties nickname him Adversary. "Nevertheless, now you had better stop your idle prattle and observe and listen to what is to take place, " he added. "Very well, " I replied, " I shall gladly do so."

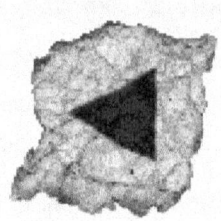  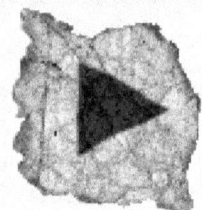

CHAPTER XXXI

SOLOMON, WITH GREAT RETINUE, COMES TO THE PALACE OF WISDOM

SOLOMON STEPPED FORTH WISHING TO OBTAIN WISDOM FOR HIS SPOUSE. As I was getting ready to give attention to what might take place, there suddenly arose a great noise and tumult, and when all turned around, I also looked; and I saw a person entering the palace, radiant with splendor, with a crown on his head, a golden sceptre in his hand, and followed by such an immense retinue that the very sight almost struck terror in all observers. The eyes of all, as well as mine, turned upon him. He stepped forth and announced that he had been honored by the highest God of Gods that he might examine the world with more freedom than any who had ever been before him or were to come after him and he was to take Wisdom, the ruler of the world, for his wife; and therefore came to seek her. (The name of this man was Solomon, and he was the king of the most glorious nation under the sky, Israel.)

2 WHAT WAS THE ANSWER AND WHAT DID HE SAY, ECCL.1.17. Thereupon, he was answered through the Chancelloress Prudence, that Wisdom was the wife of God Himself and could not give herself to another; but if the king wished to enjoy her good will, it would not be denied him. "Permit me to seat myself here and observe the differene between wisdom and folly." Solomon requested, "for all that is wrought under the sun is grievous unto me."

3 THE PILGRIM REJOICED. Hearing these words, Oh, how I rejoiced that at last, God willing, I should find a more reliable leader and adviser than I had hitherto. With him I hoped to be more secure and to be able to investigate all things more accurately, and I resolved that wherever he would go, I would follow; for this I began to praise God within myself.

4 SOLOMON'S COMPANY. Solomon was accompanied by a numerous retinue of servants and friends who came, along with him, to examine Wisdom, the Queen of the world; at his side were honorable men of a venerable and serious mien who, (when I asked them) were designated as patriarchs, prophets, apostles, and confessors. In the farther group I was shown some philosophers, such as Socrates, Plato, Epictetus, Seneca, and others. Then all this company seated itself along the walls and I also took my seat, eagerly awaiting what was to follow.

CHAPTER XXXII

THE PILGRIM OBSERVES THE SECRET JUDGEMENTS AND THE GOVERNMENT OF THE WORLD

I soon realized that the business transacted here had to do only with the general public policies affecting in common all the callings in the world; particular business was transacted in the appropriate headquarters, such as city-halls, courts of justice, consistories, and so forth. Let me relate as briefly as possible what took place in my presence.

2 COMPLAINTS REGARDING THE DISORDERS OF THE WORLD. First of all, Industry and Fortune, the viceregents of the world, stepped forth and brought complaints regarding the disorders afflicting all classes that were caused by mutual distrust, craftiness, deceit, and falsehoods of all kinds; petitioning that they be somehow rectified. I rejoiced to find these officials themselves now to admit the evil which I had found, namely that there was no order in the world. Perceiving this, my interpreter remarked: "You thought that you alone possessed eyes, while everybody else was blind; here you witness how diligently they watch whom such oversight is committed." "I am glad to hear it," I replied, "may God grant that a way be found to remove these evils."

3 SEARCH FOR THE CAUSES. Then the counsellors came together, as I saw, and after a short consultation, inquired through the Chancelloress Prudence whether it were possible to discover who caused these evils. After much investigation it was announced that certain rioters and ruffians had slipped into the country and were spreading both private and public disosrders. Among these the chief blame was laid on Drunkenness, Greed, Usury, Lust, Pride, Cruelty, Laziness, and Idleness (for they were thus mentioned by name) as well as upon several others.

4 A DECREE AGAINST THE CAUSERS OF DISORDERS. After an inquiry about these individuals had been made, a decree was finally composed and read, and public proclamations (posted and displayed in public places and sent out throughout the kingdom) made it know that her Majesty, Queen Wisdom, having taken notice of certain foreigners who had surreptitiously slipped into the country and had become the cause of many disorders, were in consequence forever proscribed from all communitiese of the kingdom, namely Drunkenness, Greed, Usury, Lust and so forth, and were ordered, under penalty of death, from the hour of proclamation of the decreee, to be seen no more. When this decree was made public, it created an incredibly widespread commotion among the joyous people, for everybody (myself included) expected that the golden age of the world had begun.

5 NEW COMPLAINTS AND NEW DECREES. Within a short time, however, when no improvement was noticeable anywhere in the world, many rushed to complain that the edict had not been enforced. Thereupon, after the counsellors again gathered in council, the Queen appointed a commission which consisted of Careless and Overlook, to whom, for the greater honor, Moderation was added from among the Queen's counsellors. This commission was ordered to ascertain diligently whether the infamous banished ruffians had not remained in the country despite the edict, or whether perchance they had not the audacity to return again. The commissioners departed and returning after a time reported that they had indeed found some suspicious-looking individuals, but upon examination had found that they did not profess themselves as belonging to the banished band and, besides, that they had borne different names. Thus one resembling Drunkenness was called Tipsiness alias Joviality; another resembling Greed bore the name of Thrift ; the third, bearing a likeness to Usury was known as Interest; the fourth, resembling Lust was called Favor; the fifth, much like Pride, was known as Dignity ; the sixth, not unlike Cruelty, was called Strictness; the seventh, bearing a likeness to Laziness, was named Amiability; and so forth.

6 THE CHARACTERS ARE EXPOUNDED. Upon consideration of this report by the counsellors, it was decreed that Joviality was not to be confused with Drunkennes, nor should Thrift be called Greed, etc. Therefore, the suspected individuals were ordered to be set free, for the edict had no reference to them. This finding having been made public, the suspects were instantly freed and gathered about themselves a following of common people who adhered to and fraternized with them. I glanced at Solomon and his colleagues and observed them shaking their heads; but since they preserved their silence, so did I, although I overheard one of them whisper to another: "Only the names are proscribed; the traitors and destroyers themselves, having changed their names, have a free hand; nothing good will come of this."

7 THE ESTATES OF THE WORLD DEMAND GREATER LIBERTIES. Then the representatives of all the estates of the world entered, asking for an audience; having been admitted, they presented,with many a quaint obeisance, a humble petition of the faithful subjects of her Majesty, the most illustrious Queen, begging her graciously to remember their faithful and loyal adherence to her sceptre hitherto, and reminding her that they had ever remained content with her laws, regulations, and

her rule generally, and intended to remain so in the future; but they petitioned her Majesty the Queen for an increase of their privileges and liberties (if it might meet with Her Majesty's pleasure) as a reward for their former faithfulness, and as an incentive for continuing therein. In consideration of such benefits, they pledged their gratitude and unswerving obedience. Having finished their harangue, they bowed down to the floor and stepped back. I rubbed my eyes: "What will now follow? Does not the world possess enough privileges that it seeks for more? A bridle for you, a bridle and a whip, together with a pinch of +77hellbore!" But all this I thought to myself, having determined not to speak aloud; for it was not proper that I should do so in the presence of those wise men and greybeards who likewise witnessed the accident.

CHAPTER XXXIII

SOLOMON REVEALS THE VANITIES OF DECEPTIONS OF THE WORLD

ECCL 1,2.15: THE MASK OF WORLDLY WISDOM IS UNCOVERED. Thereupon Solomon, who had been hitherto sitting quietly, observing everything, could contain himself no longer, and cried out with a loud voice: "Vanity of vanities, all is vanity! Can that which is crooked be made straight? and can the deficiencies be+83numbered?" Then rising, and with a great tumult, followed by all his retinue, he went directly to the throne of the Queen (for neither was the fierce Warner nor the two guards able to prevent his approach; they were intimidated by his shouting and his briliance, as was the Queen and her counsellors). He stretched out his hand and tore the veil from her face; the veil, although at first it seemed costly and splendid, was found to be nothing but a spider's web. And behold, her face appeared blanched and bloated, with painted rouge spots on her cheeks, as was apparent from the fact that they peeled off in places; her hands were scabby, her entire body loathsome and her breath mephitic. The entire company, myself included, was terrified at the sight and stood as if paralysed.

2 ALSO HER COUNSELLORS ARE UNMASKED. Solomon then turned toward the counsellors of the pretended Queen and tore their masks off as well: "I perceive that instead of Justice , Injustice reigns, " he cried, "and in the place of Holiness, Abomination. Your Caution is Suspicion; your Prudence is Cunning ; your Affability is Flattery ; your Truth is a mere Appearance: your Zeal is Fury, your Valor is Foolhardiness ; yuor Love is Lust ; your Labor is Slavery ; your Knowledge is Conjecture; your Religion is Hypocrisy. Are you worthy to rule the world on behalf of Almighty God? He will bring every act into judgement, with every hidden thing, whether it be good or +84evil. But I will go and proclaim to all the world that it no longer permit itself to be led astray and beguiled."

3 SOLOMON PROCLAIMS THE VANITY OF THE WORLD THROUGHOUT THE ENTIRE WORLD. And turning, he departed in anger, followed by his retinue; but when he began to cry out in the streets, "Vanity of vanities, all is vanity!" nations and peoples of various languages, kings and queens from distant lands gathered about him from all directions; and pouring out his eloquence before them, he taught them. For his words were like goads and like firmly driven +85nails.

4 THE COUNSEL AGAINST SOLOMON IN ORDER TO OUTWIT HIM. I did not follow him, however, but remained standing with my horror-stricken guides at the palace to see what was to follow--thererupon, the Queen recovering her stupefaction, immediately consulted with her counsellors as to what should be done. Then Zeal, Earnestness, and Valor urged that the entire force should be mobilized and sent straightway in pursuit of Solomon that he might be seized. But Prudence advised, on the contrary, that no good would come from the use of force, for not only was he himself powerful, but he had drawn almost the whole world after him (as couriers, returning one after another, reported). She advised him that Affability and Craftiness, taking with them Delight from the Castle of Fortune, be dispatched after him, and whenever they found him, should by flattery win him by exhibiting and extolling the beauty, glory, and charms of this kingdom. It might be possible to ensnare him in some such way; otherwise she professed to know of no other way whatever. This advice was approved and the three were adorned to set out at once.

CHAPTER XXXIV

SOLOMON BEGUILED AND SEDUCED

SOLOMON RAINS FORTH WISDOM. Seeing this, I begged my guides to allow me to see what was going to happen. Mr. Ubiquitous consented at once and we set out with the interpreter. We found Solomon with his retinue in the street of the learned, where he was expounding, to the general astonishment, the nature of plants, beginning with the cedars of Lebanon down to the moss growing on the +87wall; similarly he taught them about beasts, birds, reptiles, and fishes, as well as about the fundamental nature of the world, the power of the elements, the arrangment of the stars, the power of human thought, and so forth. Men from all nations came to listen to his wisdom. He gained surpassing fame thereby, so that he began to feel pride in himself; particularly when Affability and Craftiness, insinuating themselves carefully among his company, began to extol his virtues before all men.

2 HE INVENTS CRAFTSMANSHIP. He then rose up and set out to investigate the other parts of the world; and entering the street of craftsmen and examining their work, he was delighted with their various arts, and, he himself with his great ingenuity invented extraordinary methods pertaining to the scientific care of gardens, orchards, and fishponds as well as to the building of houses and cities. In general, he busied himself with the increase of all human comfort.

3 HE IS ENTANGLED INTO THE STATE OF MATRIMONY. When, however, he finally entered the matrimonial street, crafty Delight met him with a company of the most charming maidens, wearing gorgeous dresses and accompanied with melodious music. A few of the most exquisite beauties welcomed him with great honor, calling him the light of humankind, the crown of the nation of Israel, and the ornament of the world: as the learned class and craftsmen--they continued--had gained much knowledge and enlightenment from the effulgence of his presence, so also the married state hoped to gain benefit from his glory. Having made a courteous reply, Solomon announced that he decided to honor the matrimonial state by participating in it; thereupon, selecting from the whole group of maidens one who seemed to him the best suited to his station (she was called the Pharaoh's daughter), he was weighed and fettered with her. But having been fascinated by her beauty, he spent more time dallying and lovemaking with her than in his labors of wisdom. Moreover (something I should have never expected) he began to cast amorous glances at the crowd of other sportive young maidens, (of whom crafty Delight brought an ever increasing number before his eyes). and having been captivated by the beauty and the charm of one after another, he took to himself the choicest wherever he found them, even dispensing with the weighing ceremony; hence, in a short time seven hundred of them were seen about him, and besides these, three hundred of the unattached; he regarded it part of his glory to surpass even in this regard all who had been before him or were to come after him. Thereafter, nothing but frivolity of all kinds was to be witnessed in his company, so that his own people were soon saddened and sighed over it.

4 HE ENTIRELY LAPSED INTO THE STATE OF IDOLATRY. He and his following then crossed the street to that of the religious; for he permitted himself to be drawn wherever his wretched company to which he was fettered dragged him. There he amused himself, along with his companions among animals and reptiles, dragons and poisonous +88 worms.

CHAPTER XXXV

SOLOMON'S COMPANY IS DISPERSED, CAPTURED, AND PUT TO GRUESOME DEATH

SOLOMON'S COMPANIONS INCENSED. Seeing him so deluded, the most eminent among his retinue, such as Moses, Elijah, Isaiah, and Jeremiah, were greatly incensed, protesting before heaven and earth that they would have no part in such abominations and admonishing the whole company to leave such vanities and follies. But because not a few still followed Solomon's example, they grew more zealous in their denunciations and thundered still more fiercely: especially Isaiah, Jeremiah, Baruch, Stephen, and Paul. Besides, Moses began to gird on his sword, Elijah to call fire from heaven and Hezekiah to order the silly idols to be destroyed.

2 THEIR DISREGARD FOR FLATTERY. When those who had been sent out to seduce Solomon, Affability, Craftines, and Delight, saw this, they associated with themselves a few philosophers, such as Mammon and others, and confronting the denunciators, exhorted them not to forget themselves, and to act with greater moderation; since the wisest of men, Solomon, submitted his mind and accommodated himself to the customs of the world, as all could see, why should they stand apart and insist on playing the wiseacre? The protesters paid no heed; but seeing that Solomon's example continued to seduce and delude many, they became still more zealous and ran about, shouting and shrieking; which caused an immense uproar.

3 PUBLIC UPRISING AGAINST THEM. The Queen, having been notified by her emissaries, sent out proclamations by which she instigated a public uprising. Then naming her bodyguard Force her commander-in-chief, she ordered, as a spectacle for all, the seizure and punishment of those rebels. The alarm was sounded and a multitude quickly gathered, ready for the combat, they were recruited not only from among the soldiers but also from among the ruling class, officials, village elders, judges, craftsmen, philosophers, physicians, jurists and even the priests, indeed, even women who were clad in a great variety of costumes and were armed with different kinds of weapons; (for they said that against such public rebels who threatened the world, everybody, whether young or old, must assist). Seeing the rushing armies, I inquired of my interpreter: "What will happen now?" "You will learn what happens to those who by their philosophizing stir up riots and storms in the world!" my interpreter answered.

4 BATTLE, SEIZURE, MURDER, BURING AND OTHER TORTURES. All at once the armies fell upon the company, attacking one here, another there, then a third, a tenth; they struck and cut, felled, trampled, seized, and bound, according to the particular fury of each assailant, and dragged them off to prison: at which my heart almost burst with pity. But fearing their ferocity, I refrained from uttering the slightest sound, and trembled all over. I saw that some of those captured and fallen stretched out their clasped hands, and begged forgiveness for their deeds: but others, the more cruelly they were treated, the more firmly they held to their convictions. Some of them were cast into fire before my very eyes, others were thrown into water, or hanged, beheaded, stretched on a cross, torn with pincer, sawed asunder, pierced, hacked, roasted on gridirons. Nor am I able to enumerate all the gruesome kinds of death which they suffered, while multitudes of worldly people exulted and shouted with glee at the sight.

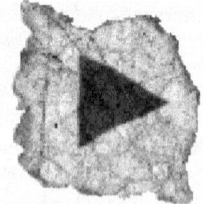

CHAPTER XXXVI

THE PILGRIM DESIRES TO FLEE FROM THE WORLD

THE PILGRIM FLEES THE WORLD. Being unable to look upon it any longer or to bear the pain in my heart, I fled, desiring to seek refuge in some desert, or rather, if it were possible, to escape from the world altogether. But my guides set out after me and catching up with me, demanded to know where I was fleeing. Wishing to repulse them by silence, I answered not a word. But when they obstinately importuned me, determined not to let me go, I exclaimed: "I already clearly perceive that it is useless to expect better things in the world. My hope is dead. Woe is me!" "Are you never to recover your sense, even after witnessing such examples as you have seen?" they retorted. "I choose rather to die a thousand times, " I answered, "than to remain here where such things occur and to look upon wrong, fraud, lie, guile, cruelty. Therefore, I prefer death to life; I go to see the lot of the dead whom I observe being borne out."

2 MR. DELUSION DISAPPEARED. Mr. Ubiquitous at once consented, saying that it was well to see and understand even that, but my other companion did not advise it, in fact, opposed it. I paid no attention to him and tearing myself away, went on. He remained behind and left me."

3 THE PILGRIM SEES THE DYING AND THE DECEASED. Thereupon, looking around, I observed the manner of the dying, of whom there were plenty about me. I saw a sorry spectacle, for every one gave up his spirit and terror, lamentations, fear and trembling, not knowing what would become of him afterwards nor where he would find himself after leaving the world. I likewise feared it, but nevertheless desiring to understand it a littlebetter, I walked between the rows of biers until I reached the end of the world and of light; there the friends of the deceased closed their eyes and blindly hurled their dead into the abyss. Casting off the glasses of delusion and rubbing my eyes, I leaned out as far as I could. There I saw nothing but frightful darkness and gloom of which neither the bottom nor the end could be fathomed by the human mind, and in which nothing but worms, frogs, serpents, scorpions, pus and stench were found; besides, a smell of brimstone and pitch, overpowering the body and the soul, issued thence, in a word, horror unspeakable!

4 THE PILGRIM FAINTED, TERRIFIED. All my innermost parts were paralysed, and trembling all over and terror-stricken, I fell fainting to the ground. "Oh, thrice miserable, wretched, unhappy men!" I cried out in anguish, "is this your ultimate glory? Is this the conclusion of so many of your splendid deeds? Is this the goal of your learning and the manifold wisdom with which you are so puffed up? Is this the desired peace and rest after your innumerable labors and struggles? Is this the immortality which you forever promise yourselves? Oh, that I had never been born! That I had never passed through the gate of life, if ather all the futilities of the world I am to become a prey to this darkness and horror! Oh, God, God, my God! If Thou exist, O God, have pity upon me, a wretched man!"

CHAPTER XXXVII

THE PILGRIM FINDS HIS WAY HOME

THE FIRST CONVERSION IS THE WORK OF GOD. When I ceased speaking, but still continued to tremble all over with terror, I heard a still small voice behind me, whispering: "Return!" I lifted my head and looked around to see who was calling me and where he commanded me to return; but I saw no one, not even my guide, Mr. Ubiquitous. For even he had left me.

2 Then, lo! the voice again sounded: "Return!" Not knowing whither to return, nor how to find my way out of the darkness, I felt dismayed, but the voice called a third time: "Return to the place whence you came, to the home of your heart and shut the door behind you!"

3 THE SECOND CONVERSION REQUIRES OUR OWN ENDEAVOUR AS WELL. I obeyed the counsel as I understood it, and I did exceedingly well to have thus obeyed God who was counselling me, but even that was His gift. Collecting my thoughts as well as I could, and shutting my eyes, ears, mouth, and nostrils, and all other outward passages. I entered into the inner recesses of my heart, and lo! it was dark. But after peering into it, and looking about a little, I perceived after a while a very faint light streaming in through some cracks, by which I was able to distinguish above in the vault of this my chamber a large round glass window. But it was so dirty and so thickly smeared with filth that no light could penetrate it.

4 DESCRIPTION OF CORRUPT HUMAN NATURE. Looking about me by this dim light, I discerned various pictures on the walls which, as it appeared to me, possessed once upon a time considerable beauty; but now the colors were faded and some limbs of the figures were severed or broken off. I approached closer and noticed their names: Prudence, Humility, Justice, Purity, Temperance, and so forth. In the middle of the room were scattered some damaged and broken ladders; also broken pulleys and pieces of ropes. Besides, I saw large wings with plucked feathers, as well as clock-wheels or bent cylinders, teeth, and rods, all scattered pell-mell.

5 WORLDLY WISDOM CANNOT MEND IT. I wondered what the purpose of these various instruments was and how and by whom they had been damaged: and how they could be repaired. But looking and considering I could think of nothing; nevertheless, I began to hope that he who had led me into this chamber by his call--whoever he might be--would make himself heard again and would direct me what else to do. For I began to be pleased with the beginnings of what I saw: the chamber did not have the offensive stench of those other places which I had visited in the world, neither did I hear the noise and clatter, the din and crash, the disquiet and whirl, the tugging and violence, (of which the world was full) for all was quiet here.

CHAPTER XXXVIII

HE RECEIVES CHRIST AS HIS GUEST.

OUR ILLUMINATION COMES FROM ABOVE. I considered these things within myself, and awaited what would follow. Behold! a bright light burst upon me from above. I looked up and saw the upper window full of dazzling light, in which brilliance I saw a man, in outward appearance like unto us men, but in his effulgence, truly God, descending toward me. His face, though dazzlingly light, could yet be looked upon with the human eye; nor was it terrifying. On the contrary, such loveliness radiated from it as I had never experienced anywhere in the world. He then, all kindly, all benign, addressed me in these most gracious words.

2 THE SOURCE OF ALL LIGHT AND ALL JOY IS THERE. "Welcome, welcome, my dear son and brother!" Saying that, he embraced me affably and kissed me. He filled the air with such an exquisite fragrance that I was overcome with ineffable joy and tears gushed from my eyes; nor did I know what to reply to such an unexpected welcome, so I sighed deeply and gazed humbly at him. Seeing me so terrified with joy, he went on speaking: "Where have you been, my son? Where did you tarry so long? Where have you been wandering? What have you been seeking in the world? Happiness? Where should you have sought God but in His temple? and where is the temple of the living God but the living temple which He has prepared for Himself, your own heart? I have watched you, my son, while you were straying, but I did not wish to see you stray any longer, and have brought you to me by leading you into yourself. For here have I chosen a palace for my dwelling; and if you dwell with me, you will find here all that you sought in vain in the world--peace, happiness, glory, and an abundance of all good things. I promise you, my son, that here you shall not be disappointed as you have been in the world."

3 TOTAL CONSECRATION TO GOD. Hearing this speech and surmising that this was my Savior, Jesus Christ, of whom I had heard something even in the world, I clasped my hands joyfully and trustfully--not as formerly, fearfully and doubtfully--and stretched them toward Him. "Here I am, my Lord Jesus, take me to Thyself, " I cried. "Thine I desire to be and to remain forever. Speak to Thy servant and grant that I may obey; reveal what Thou wilt, and grant that I may find pleasure in it; lay on me what Thou pleasest, and grant that I may bear it; use me in whatever task Thou desirest, and grant that I may not fail Thee: command what Thou pleasest, and what Thou commandest, grant; may I be nothing, that Thou alone mayest be all in all."

CHAPTER XXXIX

THEIR MUTUAL ENGAGEMENT

GOD DIRECTS OUR ERRORS AS WELL. "I accept this from you, my son!" he answered, "stand fast in it, live as mine, bear my name, and remain my own. Indeed you have been and are mine from all eternity, but you did not know it before. Long ago have I prepared the happiness for you to which I shall now lead you, but you did not understand it. I have led you to myself by strange paths, through byways and turns, but you knew it not, nor did you comprehend what I, the guide of all my elect, have meant thereby; for you have not perceived my work upon you. Nevertheless, I have been with you always and have led you in such devious byways in order that I might bring you so much the closer to myself. Neither the world, nor your guides, nor Solomon, could teach you anything, nor enrich you, nor satisfy you, nor fulfill the desires of your heart; for that which you sought was not to be found in them. But I shall teach you everything, enrich you, and satisfy you."

2 ALL WORLDLY STRIVING SHOULD BE TRANSFERRED TO GOD. "This only I request of you: that whenever you have seen in the world and in all human efforts for the attainment of temporal well-being, you would transfer and turn to me, let that be your work and occupation as long as you live; then that which men seek in the world without finding it, such as peace and joy, I will give you in abundance."

3 ONLY CHRIST, THE ETERNAL SPOUSE, SHOULD BE JOINED. "You have seen in the married state how those who fall in love leave everything else in order that they might belong to each other; do likewise with me, abandon everything, even your own self, and give yourself wholly to me, and you will be mine, and it shall be well with you. Until you have done that, I assure you that you will seek peace of mind in vain; for everything in the world changes, no matter what your mind or desire may set themselves to attain, save myself; all else brings but toil and discontent, and finally will forsake you, and the delight which you had in it will turn to grief. Therefore, I advise you faithfully, my son, give up all things and cling to me alone, become mine and I yours! Let us shut ourselves together in this keep, and you will experience truer delights than could be found in an earthly marriage. Seek to please me alone, to have me for your counsellor, guide, witness, companion, and comrade in all your affairs. And whenever you speak to me, say, 'I only and Thou, my Lord'; to care for a third person is not necessary. Cling only to me, gaze only on me, converse sweetly with me, embrace me, kiss me, and in turn expect all these things from me."

4 THE ONLY GAIN SHOULD BE CHRIST HIMSELF. "You have observed in the second group with what infinite toil men seeking profit encumber themselves, what underhanded methods they employ and what dangers they risk. Deem all this drudgery as useless, knowing that but one thing is needful: the favor of God. Therefore, keeping to the one task which I have entrusted you, do your work faithfully, sincerely, and quietly, leaving to me the end and the goal of it all."

5 A MAN MUST LEARN HOW TO KNOW CHRIST. "Among the learned you have seen how they tried to fathom all things; let the summit of all your learning be to search for me in my deeds to see how wonderfully I direct you as well as all else; here you will find more material for your consideration, and that with ineffable delight, than those scholars. Instead of all libraries, to read which is endless toil and but small profit, often harm, always weariness and sorrow, I give you this one book in which are deposited all the liberal arts. Here your grammar will consist in the contemplation of my words; your dialectics in the faith in them; your rhetoric, in prayers and sighs; your natural sciences, in the examination of my works; your metaphysics, in the delight in me and in things eternal; your mathematics, in the counting, weighing, and measuring of my blessings on the one hand, and of the ungratefulness of the world on the other; your ethics, in my love which is to be the rule of all your conduct both toward me and toward your neighbors. But seek in all these arts not to be seen of men, but rather to come closer to me. For the humbler you are, the more proficient in the arts you will become. For my light illumines none but the humble heart."

6 HOW TO RECOGNIZE CHRIST AS THE BEST PHYSICIAN. "You have observed among the physicians their search for various remedies for the safeguarding of health and the prolongation of life; but why should you be anxious about how long you will live? Is it in your power? You did not enter the world at will, and you will not leave it at will, for that is governed by my providence. Be sure, therefore, that you live well, and I shall take care of how long you should live. Live humbly and sincerely according to my will, and I will be your physician; indeed, I will be your life and the length of your days. For without me even medicine is poison; when I command it, even poison must effect a cure. Therefore, commend your life and your health to me and give yourself no further concern about them."

7 AS COUNSELLOR GUIDE AND ADVOCATE. "You have observed in the legal profession the strange and tortuous quibblings by which men have been taught to contend with each other about their various disputes. Let these be your legal maxims:

envy no one his property nor deny him your own, but leave every one to his possessions and do not withhold from him your own where he has need of it; pay all your obligations, and if you can benefit anyone beyond your obligations, regard it as your debt to do so; for the sake of peace give up all, even yourself; if anyone would take away your coat, give him your cloak also, and if he would strike you upon one cheek, turn to him also the other. These are my legal maxims; and if you observe them, you are certain of preserving peace."

8 WHAT THE RELIGION OF CHRIST IS. "You have observed in the new world how men in performing their religious duties indulge in ceremonies and quarrel over them. Let your religion consist in serving me quietly, and in being free from bondage to ceremonies, for I do not require them of you. And when you serve me as I teach you, in spirit and in truth, do not contend with anyone if he should call you a hypocrite, a heretic, or what not; but cling quietly to me and preserve in my service."

9 AND HOW HIS KINGDOM IS ADMINISTERED. "Among the rulers and governors of human societies you have observed how men like to push themselves into the chief places and to rule others. But you, my son, as long as you live, seek the lower places and desire to obey rather than to command. It is easier, safer, and more comfortable to stand behind others than in the forefront. But if you still want to rule and to command, rule your own self; I entrust your body and soul, instead of a kingdom, into your keeping; you have there as many subjects as there are members of your body and impulses of your soul; seek to rule them so that all may be well. But if my providence be pleased to entrust you with something more, go obediently and do faithfully what I command; not because of your inclination, but because of my call."

10 AND WHAT THE WARS ARE. "In the military class you have seen that heroism consists in the destruction and plunder of one's own kind. But I direct you to oppose other enemies against whom from this moment you must strive to prove your heroism: namely, the devil, the world, and your own carnal desires. Guard yourself against these as best you can; the former two drive away, and the latter one strike and kill; if you acquit yourself valiantly in this warfare, I promise you truly that you shall obtain a more glorious crown than this world can grant."

11 IN CHRIST ALONE THERE IS ABUNDANCE OF ALL. "You have likewise observed what men have sought in the castle of pretended happiness, and what they delighted in: wealth, pleasure, and glory. But you care for none of these things: for they give you no peace but rather unrest, and are the path to sorrow. Why should you care for great wealth? Wherefore should you desire it? Life's necessities are but few and it is my concern to watch over everyone who serves me. Therefore seek to gather the inner treasures, enlightenment, and piety, and all those other things shall I add unto you. For heaven and earth shall be yours by hereditary right, I assure you. Neither will these treasures rot and oppress you, as is the case with the others, but will give you unspeakable delight."

12 THE MOST DEAR COMPANIONSHIP IS THERE. "In this world men gladly seek companionship, but as for you, avoid all noisy crowds and cultivate solitude. Company is but an aid to sin, or to trivialities, idleness, or waste of time. Do not fear that you are alone, even though you should be solitary; for I am with you, as well as the host of my angels, and you may have communion with us. Moreover, if at times you should desire some visible companionship, be sure to associate with men of the same spirit, so that your conversation may be for your mutual confirmation in God."

13 THERE IS DELIGHT. "Worldly men find their joy in an abundance of feasts; in eating, drinking, and laughter; let your delight be in hunger, thirst, and weeping, if need be, and in the bearing of blows and of all other afflictions, for my sake or with me. But if I grant you a life of comfort, you may rejoice in it (although not for its own sake indeed, but rather for my sake and in me)."

14 THERE IS GLORY. "You have seen that worldlings aspire after glory and honor; but you care not for a reputation among men. Whether they speak well or ill of you, let it be of no concern to you, provided I am satisfied with you. Knowing that you are pleasing to me, care not to be pleasing to men, their favor is fickle, incomplete, and perverse; they often love what is worthy of hatred, and hate what is worthy of love. Nor is it ever possible to please them all: seeking to please one, you displease others. Therefore it is best for you to leave them all and to cleave to me alone; if we remain in mutual accord, the tongues of men will neither add nor detract anything from you or from me. Seek not to be known by many, my son; but make lowliness your fame, so that, if possible, the world may know nothing about you; this is the best and the safest way. My angels, meanwhile, will know you and will speak about you, will watch your course and, if need be, will proclaim your deeds on earth as well as in heaven; of that be assured. Of course, when the time of reification of all things shall come, all you who have surrendered yourselves to me shall be brought to a glory ineffable before all the angels as well as before the world. Compared with that, all worldly glory is but a shadow."

15 HERE IS THE SUMMIT OF ALL. "Briefly, my son, I say: if you possess wealth, learning, handsome appearance, wit, favor of men, or any other thing deemed excellent in the world, do not on that account vaunt yourself; or if you have none of them, care not for it; but leaving all these external things, whether you or others possess them, have your communion with me

here, inwardly, within yourself. Thus freeing yourself from all creatures and giving up and renouncing even your own self. I promise that you shall find me, and in me the fullness of peace."

16 TOTAL CONSECRATION TO CHRIST IS THE MOST BLESSED THING. "Lord, my God, now I understand that Thou alone art all in all," I exclaimed, "he who has Thee can easily dispense with the whole world, for in Thee he possesses more than he can ask for. Now I understand that I had gone astray while loitering through the world, seeking rest in created things. From this hour, I desire no other delight but Thee, and surrender myself wholly to Thee. Strengthen me, lest I fall away from Thee to created things, committing again the folly of which the world is full. May Thy grace protect me, for I rely on it alone."

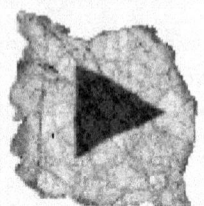

CHAPTER XL

HOW THE PILGRIM WAS TRANSFORMED

DESCRIPTION OF THE REBIRTH. While I was speaking, the light about me began to increase and I perceived that those pictures, which I had formerly seen faded and broken, became whole, clearly observable, and beautiful. Indeed, they began to move before my eyes. Likewise, the scattered and broken wheels were assembled into one whole and produced a wonderful instrument, like a clock, manifesting the courses of the world and God's marvelous government of it. The ladders, leading up to the window through which the heavenly light was streaming, were also repaired, and I understood that by means of them I could peer out into the beyond. The plucked wings which I had observed previously now received new and large feathers, and the Lord who had spoken with me took them and fastened them to my back. "My son, I dwell in two places, " he said, "in the glory of my heaven and in the contrite heart on earth. Hence, I desire that you also should have two habitations; one here at home, where I have promised to dwell with you, and the other with me in heaven. I give you these wings (which are the desire of eternal +99things) that with them you may reach heaven; you will be able, whenever you wish, to lift yourself up to me, that we may have delight in each other."

  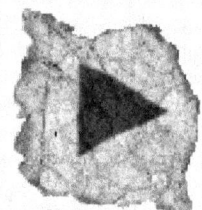

CHAPTER XLI

THE PILGRIM IS DIRECTED TO THE INVISIBLE CHURCH

NEW BRIDLE AND EYEGLASSES. "In the meantime, for your strengthening and fuller understanding of that consolation to which I have called you, I send you among my other servants who have previously abandoned the world and have surrendered themselves to me, so that you may observe their conduct." "Where do they dwell, my Lord?" I inquired, "where shall I seek them?" He answered: "They live scattered among the others in the world, but the world knows them not. In order that you may distinguish them and that you may be secure against the wiles of the world while you remain in it until I recall you out of it, and in place of the glasses and the bridle which you wore formerly, I place upon you my own yoke, (which is obedience to me) so that you may ever after follow none but myself. Besides, I add these glasses through which you will be able to discern still more clearly the futilities of the world, in case you should look at them, as well as the consolation of my elect." (The rim of the glasses was the Word of God, and lenses were the Holy Spirit.) "Go now, " he continued, "and return to the place that you by-passed previously, there you will see things which you would not have perceived at the time without the aid of these gifts of mine."

2 THE TRUE CHRISTIANS IN THE MIDST OF THE PRETENDING ONES AND WHEREIN THEY DIFFER. I recalled where I had passed by the place spoken of and arising, hastened back to it with such eagerness that I did not even notice the turmoil of the world about me. Thereupon I entered the temple called Christianity, and espying in the innermost part of the chor a curtain or a screen, I went directly toward it, not even glancing at the quarreling sects along the sides. It was then for the first time that I realized what that corner was: namely, that it was called praxis christianismi, the truth of Christianity. The curtain which separated it from the rest was twofold: the outward, which could be seen from the outside, called contemptus mundi, the contempt of the world, was darker in color; the other, inner curtains was resplendent, and was called amor Christi, the love of Christ; these two curtains, I observed, separated and divided this place from the rest; but the inner was not visible from the outside. Anyone who entered through the curtain at once became different from other people, being full of bliss, joy, and peace.

3 THERE ARE FEW CHRISTIANS, AND WHEREFORE? While standing outside and looking about, I saw an astounding and puzzling phenomenon: that although many thousands of people were constantly passing by the place, they did not enter it; whether they did not see it or simply ignored it because of its outward unprepossessing appearance, I do not know. I saw many learned in the Scriptures, priests and bishops, as well as many others who had pretentions to sanctify, pass by and some of then even as much as peep in, but they did not enter: which made me pity them. Some of them, approaching closer, noticed a ray of light through a crevice or perceived a sweet fragrance issuing thence, which attracted them, so that they began to search for the entrance. But even among these, who began to look for the door, some turning back, were struck by the dazzling flash of the world and went away.

4 NECESSITY OF REBIRTH. But I perceived the real reason why so few entered when I approached the door of the partition: for a most rigorous examination was held there. All those wishing to enter were required to surrender all their possessions, and even their eyes, ears, mind and heart; for, they said, he who aspires to be wise in God's sight must become simple in his own; and he who wishes to know God must forget all else; and he who desires to possess God must give up everything else. Hence, those who were unwilling to abandon their wealth of their learning, contending that such things were aids to heaven, remained outside and did not enter. Those who were allowed to enter, had to submit, I noticed, to a search not only of their clothing for the least bit of vanity that might be concealed there, but also (a thing unusual elsewhere) had their inner parts, the head and the heart , examined in order that nothing unclean might defile the dwelling place of God. Although this could not be done without a certain amount of pain, yet the wound was healed so skillfully by a heavenly medicine that the operation rendered the patient's life more abundant, rather than poorer. For in place of the blood which had been spilled during the piercing and cutting operation, a kind of fire was kindled in the man's limbs which transformed him so thoroughly that he himself marvelled at the change and his willingness hither to carry such useless burdens as the world calls wisdom, glory, pleasure, and wealth (for they indeed are nothing but burdens). I beheld there the lame leap,the stutters speak eloquently, the simple shame of philosophers, and those who possessed nothing claim the possession of all things.

5 THE CHURCH IS THE WORLD UPSIDE DOWN. Having observed these preliminaries at the door, I passed within the enclosure and (at first all things in general, and then more particularly) examined some of the elect. I was filled with unspeakable joy, for I saw everything just the opposite to the conditions in the world. For in the latter I had seen blindness and darkness everythwere, here nothing but dazzling light; in the world fraud, here truth; the world had been full of disorder; here existed nothing but the most excellent order; in the world, bustle, here peace; there worry and anxiety, here joy; in the world want,

here abundance; there slavery and subjection, here liberty; in the world everything toilsome and laborious, here all was easy, there the most lamentable accidents everywhere, here perfect safety. All this I desire to discuss a little more fully.

CHAPTER XLII

THE LIGHT OF THE SPIRITUAL CHRISTIANS

THE TWO-FOLD LIGHT OF TRUE CHRISTIANS. The world and those who grope in it are guided almost exclusively by mere suspicion; in their actions one follows the example of another, in everything directing themselves by touch like blind men, now and then catching themselves or colliding. But Christians have a twofold brilliant inner light; the light of reason and the light of faith; which are guided by the Holy Spirit.

2 THE LIGHT OF REASON. For although upon entering the chamber they must lay aside and surrender their reason, it is restored to them by the Holy Spirit purified and sharpened; so that they are as if full of eyes; wherever they sojourn in the world, whatever they see, hear, smell, or taste, either above, beneath, or about them, they discern everywhere the footprint of God and know well how to turn all to the fear of God. For that reason they are wiser than all the philosophers of the world, who are blinded by God in His righteous judgement so that they do not realize that even though they profess to know everything, they know nothing; neither what they possess or do not possess; neither what they do, nor what they should do and do not do; neither what goal they strive to reach or are reaching. Their knowledge contents itself with the husk, that is, the futile scanning of the exterior; but does not penetrate the inner kernel which the all-pervading glory of God. But a Christian in everything he sees, hears, touches, smells, or tastes, he sees, hears, touches, smells, and tastes God, having assurance within himself that his experience is not a mere supposition but a real truth.

3 THE LIGHT OF FAITH. Of course, the light of faith likewise illumines him brightly, so that he may see and know not only what he looks at, hears, or touches but even the intangible and the unseen. For God has revealed in His Word what is above the heavens in the highest as well as what is beneath the earth in the abyss below, and what had been before the world and shall be after. The Christian, believing this, has all plainly before his eyes, while the world cannot grasp it. For the world will accept nothing but tangible proof, so that it believes only what it grasps in its hand: while the Christian relies so boldly upon the invisible, absent and future things that he abhors those present. The world demands proofs; the Christian rests content with the bare words of God. The world demands sureties, pledges, hostages, and seals; the Christian regards faith as sufficient for all assurance. The world suspects, probes, tests, and spies: the Christian relies entirely upon God's truthfulness. Thus, where the world always has a reason for stopping and doubting, questioning, hesitating, the Christian always has a reason to believe implicitly, to obey, to submit; for the light of faith illumines him that he may see and know that all these things are immutable and cannot be otherwise, notwithstanding his inability to grasp them by the light of reason.

4 THE WONDERS OF GOD SEEN BY THIS LIGHT, THE COURSE OF THE WORLD. Looking about me by this light, I saw an astounding and most wonderful spectacle, beyond my powers of description. I shall but adumbrate it partlky. I saw this world before me as an enormous and immense clock, composed of various visible and invisible part, but made entirely of glass, transparent and brittle; it exhibited a thousand, nay a thousand thousand larger and smaller rods, wheels, hooks, teeth, and notches, all in motion and oscillation, one within another; some moved noiselessly, others with some friction or grating. In the center was placed the principal, although invisible wheel, from which motion was transmitted in an incomprehensible way to all the rest of the machinery. For the spirit of the wheel was imparted to all the others and dominated them; and although it seemed to me impossible fully to comprehend it, nevertheless I saw plainly and distinctly that it really occurred. I was greatly astonished as well as pleased to find that although many of those wheels sometimes slipped off and fell out, for the teeth and notches and even the wheels and rods themselves were occasionally loosened and dropped out, the general movement never ceased; this was done by some mysterious contrivance of its secret diretion that restored and replaced the lost parts.

5 HOW EVERYTHING IS RULED BY THE SECRET ORDINANCE OF GOD. Let me speak more clearly: I saw the glory of God, how the heavens, the earth, and the abyss, as well as everything that could be imagined beyond the earth to the infinite reaches of eternity were filled with His powe and His Godhead. I saw, I say, that His omnipotence penetrated all things and provided the foundation for all things; everything that happens throughout the breadth of the world, in all things from the vastest to the minutest, occurs only by His will. All this I myself have seen.

6 PARTICULARLY AMONG MEN. And speaking particularly of men, I saw that all men, whether good or bad, live, move, and have their being only in God and by the power of God. For every motion and breadth of their proceed from Him and occur by His power. I beheld how His seven eyes, each a thousand times brighter than the sun, range throughout the world and note everything that happens, whether in light or in darkness, in the open or in secret, even to the profoundest depths, and penetrate into the hearts of all men. Likewise I saw His mercy which floods all His deeds, particularly in His dealings with men.

For I saw how He loves them all and seeks their good, shows forbearance to sinners, forgives transgressors, recalls the straying, receives the returning, awaits the procrastinating, patiently bears with the recalcitrant, is long-suffering wiht those who provoke Him, pardons the penitent, and embraces the obedient. He instructs the simple, comforts the sorrowing, forewarns the falling, raises the fallen, responds to those who ask and grants freely to those who ask not, opens to those who knock and of those who knock not He Himself asks admittance, permits Himself to be found by those who seek Him amd and manifests Himself to those who seek Him not.

7 FURIOUS AGAINST THE WICKED. On the other hand, I also observed His fearful and terrible fury against the rebellious and the ungrateful whom He pursues angrily in His furious wrath and overtakes them no matter where they turn: for to escape from His hand is impossible and to fall into His hand is terrible. In short, all those who surrender themselves to God see how the terror and the majesty of God reign supreme above all, so that everything from the greatest to the most insignificant takes placed by his will.

  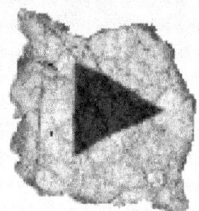

CHAPTER XLIII

THE LIBERTY OF HEARTS DEVOTED TO GOD

THE TRUE CHRISTIANS ARE UNMOVED. From this source they derive what the wisest of the world vainly seek in their endeavors--namely, the entire freedom of mind, that they may be subjected to or bound by nothing but God nor be bound to do anything contrary to their will. The world was full of coercion, all things having gone contrary to everyone's desires, each being inordinately bound either by himself or by others; hence he, having been compelled by the force of his or someone else's will, has ever been struggling either with himself or with others. On the contrary, here all is serene. For all having given themselves to God so completely that they care nothing else, acknowledge no one above themselves but God. Hence, they do not obey the commands of the world, and spurn its promises, laughing at its threats, regarding as inferior all external things because of the certainty of the value of their inward riches.

2 AND UNYIELDING. Consequently, the Christian, otherwise quite approachable, yielding, willing, and obliging, in the privilege of his heart is adamant. Hence he is bound neither to friends nor foes, nor to lord or king, neither to wife nor children, nor finally even to himself to such an extent that he feels obliged, for their sake, to recede in any way from his purpose, namely, from the fear of God, but rather strides steadfastedly forward. No matter what the world may do, say, threaten, promise, command, beg, advise, or urge, he does not permit himself to be moved.

3 THE GREATEST FREEDOM TOGETHER WITH THE GREATEST BONDAGE. The world, ever perverse, and grasping a shadow in place of the truth, imagines that liberty consists in being free, in serving no one, but in surrendering oneself to idleness, pride, and passions. On the contrary, the Christian acts far differently; for he, after fortifying well his own heart that it may preserve its freedom in God, employs all else in ministering to the needs of his fellows. For I have seen and learned that no greater servitude exists anywhere, and none is more enslaved, if I may use the expression, than the man devoted to God: for he performs willingly and gladly even the lowest menial services which one intoxicated with the world despises. Whenever he sees an opportunity to be of benefit to his fellows, he hesitates not or holds not back for a moment, pities not himself, exaggerates not the rendered, does not continually remind others of them, perseveres ever, and whether treateed with gratitude or not, quietly and joyfully keeps on serving.

4 AND WHAT A DELIGHT THIS IS. Oh, the blessed servitude of the sons of God, than which nothing freer can be imagined, in which man submits himself to God in order to be free everywhere else! Oh, the unhappy liberty of the world, than which no greater slavery can exist, in which men disregarding God permit themselves to become miserably enslaved by things! Particularly when they serve creatures over whom they should rule, and resist God when they should obey. Oh, mortals, would that we might understand that there is but One and only One who is higher than we; the Lord, our Maker and our future Judge! Who, having the power to command us, does not constrain us as slaves, but calls us as children to His obedience; desiring that even when we obey we may do so freely and unconstrainedly. Truly, to serve Christ is to reign; and to be a vassal of God is a greater glory than to be the monarch of all the earth; what then shall it be to be a friend and a child of God!

CHAPTER XLIV

THE RULE OF SPIRITUAL CHRISTIANS

GOD'S LAWS ARE BRIEF. God indeed desires to have His chilren free but not self-willed: therefore, He surrounds them with certain rules more effectively than anything similar that I could observe in the world. There, indeed, everything, was in disorder: partly because it had no definite order, and partly because men did not observe what order there was. But these who dwell within the partition, possess and observe a most excellent order. For they have rules given them by God Himself, full of justice, that decree that everyone devote to God must profess and know Him as the only God, and must serve Him in spirit and in truth, without devising for himself and carnal additions. He must employ his tongue not in offendingbut in honoring His revered name: he must spend the times and seasons appointed for His service in none but His outward and inward worship; he must be subject to his parents and others appointed over him by God; he must cause no injury to the life of his neighbor; and must preserve his own body in purity; he must respect the property of others, eschew falsehood and deceit, and must restrain his mind within the prescribedbounds and limits.

2 THEY ARE SUMMED UP IN TWO WORDS. In brief, he must love God above all which can be named and must sincerely desire as great a good for his neighbor as for himself. Which sum of God's laws, comprised in these two sentences, I have heard very highly praised, and I myself have found and tested them to be worth all the innumberable laws, enactments, and decrees of the world, yea, a thousand times superior to them.s

3 THE TRUE CHRISTIAN DOES NOT REQUIRE COPIOUS LAWS. For he who loves God with all his heart needs no prescriptions as to when, where, and how many times he must serve, worship, and honor Him. For that sincere union with God, and his readiness to obey, are themselves the most acceptable ways of honoring God and lead man to praise God through his very being and to glorify Him through all his deeds. Similarly, he who loves his neighbor as himself needs no elaborate directions as to where, when, and wherein he should have regard for him, wherein he should not injure him, and how to return the debt which is due: love will fully instruct and show him how to conduct himself toward his neighbor. It is the mark of a wicked man to demand everywhere his rights and to guide himself in his conduct towards others strictly in accordance with written rules; for as the finger of God points out to our hearts that which we desire for ourselves, we are in duty bound to deal similarly with our neighbors. But because the world ignore the inner witness of its own conscience and observes only the external regulations, there exists no rightful order in the world, but only suspicions, mistrust, misunderstandings, jealousies, quarrels, envy, hatreds, theft, murders, and what not. But those who are truly devoted to God, observe only what their conscience prompts, and whatever it forbids they do not do; whatever it shows should be done they do, irrespective of gain, favor, or any other thing.

4 THERE IS UNANIMITY AMONG TRUE CHRISTIANS. Thence follows a certain unanimity or similarity of one Christian with another, for they all are as if cast in the same mold: all think alike, believe alike, and have tastes alike, because all have been taught by the selfsame Spirit. It is remarkable--a thing that I observed with gladness--that men who have never seen or heard of each other and have been separated from one another by the breadth of the world, yet are so much alike as two peas: they speak the same things, see and feel the same as if they were one. Moreover, despite the great diversity of gifts among them, they produce a pleasing symphonic harmony, just as musical instruments do, the strings and pipes of which give out a different quality of tones, the one softer, the other louder. This is the great secret of Christian unity, in fact a proof of the divine unity and the foreshadowing of eternity, where all things will be dominated by one spirit.

5 AND COMPASSION. From this unanimity arises their mutual sympathy, so that they rejoice with those who rejoice and mourn with those who mourn. For I have remarked a most iniquitous thing in the world, which saddened me many a time: that whenever anyone fared ill, others were glad of it; whenever he strayed, they laughed at him; whenever he suffered loss, they tried to profit by it. Furthermore, they themselves caused their neighbor's downfall and loss for their own profit, entertainment, and sport. Among the Christians I found no such thing; for each tried to ward off misfortune and calamity from his neighbor as earnestly an diligently as from himself; and if he could not ward it off, he was genuinely grieved as if it affected him. As a matter of fact, it did affect him, for they are all but one heart and one soul. Just as all compass-needles, when magnetized, point in the same direction, so the hearts of these people, impregnated by the spirit of love, turn all in the same direction: in happiness to joy, in misfortune to grief. Here I have learned that those are but false Christians who attend diligently only to their own affairs and not care for their neighbors'; and adroitly turning away from the hand of God, when it presses on them, they feather only their own nests, leaving others out in the wind and the rain. A far different order have I observed here: when one suffers, the rest do not rejoice; when one is hungry, the rest do not feast; when one is engaged in a fight, the rest do not sleep; but all things are done in common, so that it is a joy to look at it.

6 AND COMMUNITY IN ALL GOOD THINGS. Concerning possessions, I observed that although the majority of them are poor, not possessing or caring for much of what the world calls riches, nevertheless almost every one of them owns some. But he does not conceal it, and as happened in the world does not hid it from the rest, but holds it as if in common, ready and williing to aid anyone and to loan it to anyone in need of it. All use their property in such a way that it is as if they sat around a common table and used the provisions with equal right. Seeing this, I felt ashamed to think that with us it often happens contrariwise, some filling and cluttering their houses with furnishings, clothes, food, gold, and silver as much as they can, while at the same time others, who are no less God's servants, have scarcely enough to eat and to put on. Then I understood, repeat, that it was by no means the will of God, but the usage of this perverse world, that some should go about in finery while others are naked; some belching with over-satiety, while others yawn with hunger; some earning laboriously, others squandering profligately; some spending their time in amusements, others in weeping. For from this follow pride and contempt of others on the part of the former, and envy, jealousy, and other passions on the part of the latter. But no such thing is found among the Chistians: for everything is common to all, even to their very souls.

CHAPTER XLV

HEARTS DEVOTED TO GOD FIND ALL THINGS LIGHT AND EASY

IT IS EASY TO OBEY GOD. Nor do they find it difficult to submit to such a rule: but on the contrary, it is their pleasure and delight. In the world, on the contrary, I saw that men conformed but unwillingly, only as they were constrained to do so. As for these, God has changed their stony hearts and given them hearts of flesh, pliable and perfectly yielding to His will. Although the devil by his crafty suggestions, the world by its influence, and the flesh by its natural disinclination toward the good have caused them difficulties, yet they care not for any of these things. They drive the devil away by the bombardment of their prayers, guard themselves against the world by the shield of their unswerving determination, and compel their body to obedience by the scourge of discipline. Thus they joyfully continue to perform their duties (within the limits of their present attainments). Thus I found that in truth to serve God with one's whole heart is not a drudgery but a delight; and I understood that those who too frequently excuse themselves on the score of being only human do not appreciate the power and effectiveness of the new birth, or perhaps have never experienced it. Let them beware! Among the Christians I found none to claim license to sin by alleging the weaknes of the flesh, or to excuse the perpetration of a vile deed by the fraility of human nature. For here I saw that whoever surrendered his entire heart to Him who had created it, redeemed it and sanctified it for His temple, found his other members, freely and by degrees, to follow the heart, and to incline toward whatever God directed. Oh, Christian, whoever you are, free yourseld from the fetters of the flesh, discover, experience, and learn that the obstacles which your mind imagines are too small to be able to obstruct your will, provided only that you will be earnest!

2 TO SUFFER FOR CHRIST IS DELIGHTFUL. Not only is it easy to do what God desires, but even to suffer what He imposes. For not a few of those here present have been buffeted, spat upon, and beaten by the world, but have wept with joy and have lifted their hands to God in praise that He has deemed them worthy to suffer for His name. So that they not only believed in the Crucified, but were themselves crucified in His honor. Others, who have been spared persecutions, envied them with a holy envy, fearing God's wrath for lack of correction and an alienation from Christ for lack of the cross. Consequently, they kissed the scourge and the rod of God whenever they were scourged by Him, and embraced every kind of cross.

3 WHENCE COMES SUCH A CONSECRATION. All this results from the complete consecration of their will to God, so that they may do nothing else or desire to become nothing else than as God has willed. Therefore, whatever befalls them, they are certain that it has come from God's providential decree. Thus nothing unexpected can overtake such men, for they count stripes, prisons, tortures, and death itself among God's good gifts. Whether they live in abundance or in want is equally indifferent to them, save that they regard the former as the more questionable, the latter the safer. Consequently, they take delight and pride in their trials,wounds, and scars. In brief, they are so seasoned in God that unless they suffer, they regard themselves as idling and wasting their time. Nevertheless, it were better not to lay hands on them rashly; for the more eagerly they expose their backs, the more difficult it is to strike them; and the more fools they seem, the more dangerous it is to ridicule them. For they belong no longer to themselves but to God, and what is done to them is regarded by God as done to Himself.s

  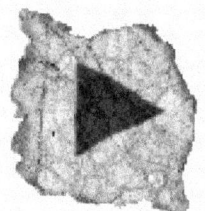

CHAPTER XLVI

THE SAINTS POSSESS AN ABUNDANCE OF ALL THINGS

TO BE CONTENT WITH WHAT ONE HAS IS TRUE WEALTH. The world is full of Marthas, hustling and bustling, intent on gathering things from all directions and caring for them, yet never having enough. These Christias, on the contrary, have a different temper: for each desires only to sit quietly at the feet of the Lord, satisfied with whatever befalls him there. They regard the grace of God dwelling in them as their truest riches and comfort themselves with that alonee. The external possessions which the world calls riches they look upon as more burden than profit, but they use them for the necessities of life--the necessities, I say. Therefore, whatever God has granted any of them, whether it be much or little, they regard as sufficient. They believe in, and fully rely upon, God's care, and thus regard it as improper to desire anything beyond what God has granted them.

2 I observed a strange phenomenon here: some had plenty of wealth, of silver, gold, crown, and sceptres (for God has even such among His own), while others almost nothing save their half-clad body, emaciated with hunger and thirst. Yet the former professed to have nothing, while the latter to have everything, and both were of an equally cheerful spirit. Then I understood that he alone is truly wealthy and lacks nothing who knows how to be content with what he has, whether it be much, little, or no money: a large, small, or no house; expensive, cheap or no clothing, many, one, or no friend, high, low, or no position, or office, or honor, or fame: in brief, to be something or nothing is equally indifferent to them in the conviction that whatever God desires for them, or leads them to, or lifts them up to, or seats them to, thus should they go, stand, or sit; all that being better than they understand.

3 TRUE CHRISTIANS DO NOT LACK ANYTHING. Oh, the blessed and most desirable abundance! How happy are they who are wealthy in such a fashion! For even though in the eyes of the world some of them may appear wretched and miserable, yet in reality they are a thousand times better provided for, even in temporal matters, than many of the worldly-rich. For the latter must protect themselves, being subject along with their riches, to a thousand accidents, in danger of losing their goods by fire, water, rust, thieves, and other exigencies. The former, having God for their guardian, ever find in Him the source of living-supply of all their needs; for He feeds them daily from His supplies, clothes them from His store, grants them for their necessities out of His treasury--if not beyond their needs, at least always what is truly needful. If His bounty is not in accordance with their own reason, it is always according to His providence in which they trust a thousand times more readily than in their own reason.

CHAPTER XLVII

THE SECURITY OF MEN COMMITTED TO GOD

ANGELS AS GUARDIANS. Although nothing seems so vulnerable and subjected to evey kind of danger as the society of the devout--they being ill-regarded, buffeted, and beaten both the devil and the world--nevertheless I saw that they were well guarded. For their group was perceptibly surrounded by a fiery wall which, when I approached it, I noted it to be moving. For it was nothing less than a circle of many thousand of thousands of angels, who made it impossible for all their enemies even to approach them. Besides, each Christian had an angel ordained and sent by God to be his guardian,whose duty it was to watch over him and protect and defend him against all manner of dangers and snares, pits and ambushes, traps and stratagems. These angels are indeed (as I myself have learned and observed) lovers of men, being their fellow-servants, particularly when they see them observe the duties for which God has created them: such they serve gladly, guarding them against the devil, wicked men, and untoward accidents, and if necessary, even carrying them in their arms to protect them from harm. Then I realized how much depends on piety, for these beautiful and pure spirits dwell only where they perceive the fragrance of virtue and are repelled by the stench of sins and of impurity.

2 ANGELS OF OUR TEACHERS. I have likewise observed (a thing not proper to conceal) another benefit derived from this invisible holy company: namely that they not only have angels as guardians, but also as teachers of the elect, to whom they often transmit secret hints and whom they teach the deep hidden mysteries of God. For since they ever look upon the face of the omniscient God, none of those things which a pious man desires to know can remain hidden from them. They, in turn, reveal what they know, with God's permission, to men, if such knowledge is needed by the elect. Hence, the heart of the devout often has a presentiment of what is happening at a distance, and finds itself sorrowful in untoward and joyful in auspicious circumstances. It follows then that through dreams and other visions, or through secret inspiration, they picture in their minds either what has happened in the past, is taking place at present, or shall come to pass in the future. From this source come the increase of the gifts of God within us, the penetrating, beneficient meditations, and the astounding inventions with which man often surpasses himself, not knowing where they have originated. Oh, the blessed school of the sons of God! This is what often brings all the wisdom of the world to utter amazement, when it sees some simple insignificant person proclaim deep mysteries and foretell future changes in the world and in the Church, as if he saw them before his eyes, and name yet unborn kings and heads of states, and predict and announce other matters which could not possibly be learned from any study of the stars or from any exercise of human ingenuity. All these things are of such great benefit that we can never sufficiently thank our protector, God, for them or ever love sufficiently those heavenly teachers. Let us, however, return to the security of the devout.

3 GOD IS A SHIELD OF THF DEVOUT. I saw that each one of them was surrounded not only by the angelic protection, but also by God's own august presence, so that he inspired terror in those who attempted to attack hIm without God's permission. I saw miracles performed by some who had been thrown into water, fire, or to lions and wild beasts, but had suffered no harm whatever. Some had been fiercely attacked by human brutality, having been surrounded by a horde of tyrants and hangmen with their henchmen, so that sometimes powerful kings and whole kingdoms had labored assiduously for their destruction; but they had remained unhurt and had withstood it, cheerfully walking about their business. Then I realized what it is to have God for one's shield; for when He commands His servants to accomplish certain tasks in the world, and they go about their duty courageously, He, dwelling in and about them, guards them as the apple of His eye, so that they do not succumb until their alloted task is finished.

4 THE PIOUS BOASTING OF THE GODLY. They are well aware of this divine protection and cheerfully rely upon it. I heard some of them boast that they fear not even though the shadow of death fall upon them, or the whole world be risen up an the earth cast itself into the middle of the sea, or the world be full of devils. Oh, the thrice happy security, unheard of in the world, when a man is held and protected so surely in the hand of God that he is safe from the power of other things! Let understand, ye true servants of Christ, that we have a most watchful guardian and protector--the almighty God Himself. Blessed are we!

CHAPTER XLVIII

THE DEVOUT ENJOY COMPLETE PEACE

As I had formerly had observed much confusion and toil, anxiety and care, terrors and fears everywhere and among all professions in the world, so I have now found peace of mind and good cheer in all those who have surrendered themselves to God. For they feel no terror before God, being fully conscious of the kindly disposition of His heart toward them, nor do they find anything in themselves that causes them grief: for they lack no good thing, as has already been shown, neither do they suffer discomfort on account of their circumstances, not caring anything about them.

2 DISREGARD OF THE WORLD'S DERISION. It is indeed true that the wicked world gives them no peace, but heaps spite and ridicule upon them and tears, plucks, beats, and spits upon them, trips them up, and afflicts the with worst it can devise. I saw many instances of this kind of mistreatment, but we have learned that it was done by the command of supreme Lord, for thos who wish to become good must first suffer themselves to be the laughing-stock of the world. For the nature of the world is such that what is wisdom before God is to it sheer foolishness. Thus I noticed that many who were endowed with the most splendid gifts of God were treated with contempt and ridicule, and that often even among their own. It happens sometimes, I say; but I observed that they care for nothing for the contempt, but glory in the fact that the world holds its nose in their presence as it from stench, and averts its eyes from them as from a loathsome sight, scorns them as fools, and executes them as criminals. For they have made it their password whereby they recognize each other, to be rejected by the world for Christ's sake. Furthermore, they hold that whoever cannot bear wrong cheerfully, possesses not the spirit of Christ fully. Thus regarding the matter, they encourage each other therewith. Likewise, they point out that the world may be recompensed by the bountiful goodness of God. Thus the ridicule, hatred, injury, and harm meted out to us by the world shall be turned to our profit.

3 THE TRUE CHRISTIAN IS UNCONCERNED. Then I understood why these genuine Christians do not admit of the distinction between what the worlds calls fortune and misfortune, wealth and poverty, honor and dishonor: saying, that whatever comes from the hand of God is all good, fair, and profitable. Therefore, they grieve over nothing, neither are they hesitant or evasive about anything. Whether you order a genuine Christian to govern or to serve, to command or to obey, to teach others or to be taught, to enjoy abundance or to suffer want, it is all the same to him: he will go on with the same expression of face, caring only to be pleasing to God. They say that the world is not so great that it cannot be endured, nor so precious that it cannot be dispensed with. Therefore, they are not afflicted either with the longing for, or the loss of, anything. If someone strikes them on the right cheek, they cheerfully turn to him the left also; if someone disputes with them the possession of their coat, they surrender to him their cloak also; leaving all things ultimately to God, their witness and their judge, in the assurance that all these things shall in due time be settled justly.

4 WHAT HE SEES OUTWARDLY. Neither does a devout man of God permit himself to be disquieted by the condition of the nations of the world. He indeed dislikes many things, but is not destraught or tormented thereby. What cannot forward let it fall backward; what cannot stand, let it fall; and what cannot or will not survive, let it perish. Why should a Christian torment himself over it, if his conscience be right and he has the grace of God in his heart? If men will not conform themselves to our customs, let us conform ourselves to theirs as far as our consciences permit. It is true that the world goes from bad to worse, but will our fretting improve it?

5 HE CARES NOT FOR THE QUARREL OF THE WORLD. If the mighty of this world quarrel and haggle over crowns and sceptres, so that bloodshed and devastation of lands and countries result, the enlightened Christian is not afflicted within himself even over such calamities. He maintains that it is of little or no importance who rules the world. For as the world can never destroy the Church, even if Satan himself should hold its sceptre; so, on the other hand, even if a crowned angel were to hold sway over it, it would not cease to be wordly. For even then those desiring to practice genuine piety must endure sufferings. They deem it, therefore, immaterial who occupies the throne of the world, save that when it is one of the devout (as actual experience has taught), many flatterers and hypocrites unite themselves with the company of the devout and by this admixture cause the piety of the rest to grow lukewarm. On the contrary, in times of overt persecution the pious serve God with fervent zeal. Particularly when one considers that in times of peace many hide under the pretence of general welfare, religion, honesty, and liberties, who, if they wer to be exposed, would be found to seek the kingdom, liberties, and glory not of Christ, but of themselves. A Christian, therefore, leaves such matters to take care of themselves as they can or will, being content to enjoy God and His grace within his heart.

6 ABOUT THE SUFFERINGS THAT BEFALL THE CHURCH. Neither do the temptations surrounding the Church disquiet

enlightened souls. For they know that they shall ultimately triumph. But this cannot be obtained without a victory, and a victory cannot be won without a battle, and a battle cannot be fought without enemies and without a sharp conflict with them. Therefore, they confront courageously all that befalls them or others, being certain that the victory belongs to God who conducts all things as He has predetermined them, even though rocks, mountains, deserts, seas, and chasms should obstruct His way; for, in the end they all must fall back. They also know that the raging of enemies against God must in the end contribute to His greater glory. For if a thing undertaken for the glory of God should meet with no opposition, it might be regarded as of human initiation and of human accomplishmet; but on the contrary case, the more furiously the world with all its devils offers resistance, the clearer does the power of God appear.

CHAPTER XLIX

THE DEVOUT POSSESS CONSTANT JOY IN THEIR HEARTS

A GOOD CONSCIENCE IS A PERPETUAL FEAST. Nor do they merely enjoy peace within themselves, but likewise constant joy and delight, caused by the presence and consciousness of God's love. For where God is, there is heaven; where heaven is, there is eternal joy, and where eternal joy is, there man knows not what else to desire. Compared with that, all earthly joys are but a shadow, a jest, a mockery; I am unable to describe or even to suggest it sufficiently in words. I saw and perceived, I saw and learned that to possess God with His heavenly treasures is so exceedingly glorious that all the glory of the world, its splendor and glitter cannot be compared with it. It is a thing more joyful than the world can add to or detract from. It is greater and more excellent than the world can apprehend or comprehend.

2 N.B.* For how otherwise than happy and joyous can a man be who is conscious of, and perceives within himself, such light of God, such noble inner harmony caused by the Holy Spirit, such freedom from the world and its slavery, such sure and abundant care of God for himself, such protection against enemies and accidents, and finally such constant peace, as has already been demonstrated? That is the sweetness that the world understands not; the sweetness that if anyone but taste, he must thereafter dare everything for its sake; the sweetness from which no other sweetness can entice, no bitterness can alienate, no delight can allure, no calamity, not even death itself, can deprive us.

3 Then I understood what it is that at times has impelled many of God's saints willingly to throw away honors, favor of men, possessions and wealth, that makes them equally ready to surrender the world itself, were it theirs; others, to deliver their bodies gladly over to imprisonment, scourging, and death, being ready to undergo a thousand deaths--if the world could repeat them--by water, fire, and the sword, singing amidst the tortures. Oh, Lord Jesus, how sweet thou art to the hearts that have tasted Thee! Blessed is he who understands this delight!

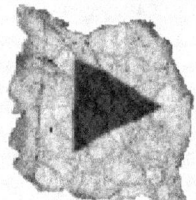

CHAPTER L

THE PILGRIM EXAMINES SOME CLASSES AMONG THE CHRISTIANS

Hitherto I have described the general characteristics of all true Christians; but perceiving among them various vocations, such as also exist in the world, I desired to examine how they conducted themselves in them. I found an excellen order in all their affairs, so that it was a joy to behold it; but I do not propose to describe it in detail. I shall touch briefly only upon a few features.

2 HOW THEIR MARRIAGE IS. Their marriage, I found, differs but little from celibacy; for there is with them a moderation both in their desires and in their attachments. Instead of the steel fetters, I saw here golden clasps; in place of tugging apart, here prevails a joyful union of their bodies and their hearts. But if, in spite of all, some lack of freedom still adheres to this state, it is outweighed by he increase of the kingdom of God which results from it.

3 WHO THEIR RULERS ARE. Those among them who are called to rule as governors, deal with the subjects committed to their care as do parents with their children--with love and care. This was pleasing to observe, and in fact I saw many lifting up their hands in gratitude to God for such rulers. On the other hand, those who are subject to the rule, seek so to live as to be subects not in word but in deed. They live thus for the sake of honoring God thereby, so that whomever He set over them, were he of whatever disposition, him they respect and honor in words, deed, and thoughts.

4 WHO THEIR LEARNED MEN ARE. Walking among them further, I saw not a few learne men who, contrary to the usage of the world, exceed others as much in humility as in learning, and are kindness and affability incarnate. I was privileged to converse with one of them of whom it was rumored that there was nothing of human learning hid from him; but he carried himself as the humblest, and lamented his lack of learning and ignorance. They esteem linguistic studies but little if wisdom is not increased thereby. They say that knowledge of languages does not impart wisdom, but is merely a medium ot communication with one or another group of the inhabitants of the world, whether living or dead. Therefore, he is not learned who can speak many languages, but rather he who can impart useful knowledge in them. They regard as useful knowledge all the works of God, to the understanding of which the liberal arts contribute somewhat , it is true, but of which the true source are the sacred Sciptures, their teacher the Holy Spirit, and the goal of it all is Christ the Crucified. Therefore, all these learned men, I observed, direct all their learning toward Him as the center; and whatever they perceive to be an obstacle to the approaching of Christ, they reject, even though it be the most ingenious. They read many books according to their needs; but they give special attention only to the choicer ones, always rating human eloquence as but human. They write book themselves, but not with the aim of making their names known, but in the hope of communicating to others something useful, and of aiding the common welfare, or defending it before an assault of evil.

5 WHO THEIR PRIESTS AND THEOLOGIANS ARE. I saw among them a certain number of priests and preachers, according to the needs of the Church, all in the simplest habit, dealing with each other as well as with the laity generally with mild and affable manners. They spend the greater part of their time with God rather than with men--in prayers, reading, and meditation.

NOTA BENE: The rest of their time they employ in instructing others either in public assemblies or privately. Their sermons--as their hearers assured me and I experienced it myself--were never heard without an inward stirring of the heart and the conscience, because of the penetrating power of divine eloquence which issues from their lips. When God's mercy or human ingratitude are discussed, I noticed both ecstasy and tears on the faces of the hearers, for the preachers' words are earnest, vital, and fervant. The preachers would regard it as shameful to teach others virtues of which they themselves are not examples, so that in their very silence there is much one can learn from them. I approached one of them wishing to speak with him; he was a person of venerable age and in his countenance shone something divine.

NOTA BENE: When he spoke to me, his words were full of kindly severity, and it was quite apparent in every way that he was God's ambassador; for there was not a whit of worldliness about him. When, according to our custom, I wished to address him by titles, he did not permit it, calling it mere worldly snobbishness and saying that it was a sufficient title and honor to be a servant of God. He bade me call him my father, if I so desired. When he bestowed his blessing upon me, I was conscious of a rapture and an expansive joy in my heart, and became aware that in truth the genuine knowledge of God--the real theology-- is more powerful and penetrating than it has generally been regarded. I blushed remembering the haughtiness of some of our priests, their pride, avarice, mutual quarrels, dislikese, and enmities, drunkenness, and in a word carnality. For their words and deeds stand so far apart that they seem to talk about virtues and Christian life only as if in jest. To tell the truth, I was pleased with these men of fervent spirit but disciplined body, lovers of heavenly things but careless of earthly, diligent over their flock but forgetful of themselves, drunk with the Spirit but not with wine, of few words but of abundant needs, each striving to be the first in work but the last in boasting: in a word, intending the spiritual upbuilding of all in their every act, word, and thought.

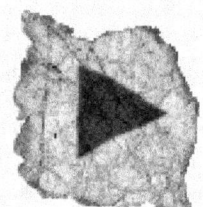

CHAPTER LI

THE DEATH OF FAITHFUL CHRISTIANS

FOR A CHRISTIAN DEATH IS PLEASANT. After having strolled sufficiently among the Christians and having examined their behavior, I finally saw that Death also moves among them. But it is not as in the world--of a hideous, naked, and repulsive appearance--but is wrapped up neatly in the linen-clothes which Christ left in His grave. Death approached one here and another there and informed them that it was time for them to depart from the world. Oh, what a joy, what a rapture was his who received this message! They submit to all manner of pain, even the sword, fire, pincers, or any other torture, only to hasten the time of their deliverance. Then each falls alseep peacefully, quietly, and gladly.

2 WHAT HAPPENS TO THEM AFTER DEATH. Watching what was to follow, I observed that the angels, according to God's command, found for each of them a spot where his body is to have its little resting chamber. When the body is placed there by friends or enemies, or even by the angels themselves, the latter guard the tomb so that the bodies of the saints are secure from Satan lest the least grain of dust should be lost. Other angels, meanwhile, taking the soul, convey it up in splendor and with wonderful raptures. When I gazed after them (adjusting my glasses), I perceived there glory ineffable.

CHAPTER LII

THE PILGRIM BEHOLDS THE GLORY OF GOD

For behold! the Lord of hosts sat upon His throne on high and about Him streamed a lightning radiance from one end of heaven to the other. His feet rested as if on crystal, emerald, and sapphire, while His throne was of jasper; over it was a beautiful rainbow. A thousand of thousands and ten thousand times hundred thousand angels stood before Him, chanting one to another: "Holy, holy, holy, the Lord of host! Heaven and earth are full of His glory!"

2 Likewise the four-and-twenty elders, falling before the throne and casting their crowns at the feet of Him who lives for ever and ever, sand with a loud voice: "Worthy art Thou, O Lord, to receive glory and honor and power; for Thou hast created all things, and they exist and were created by Thy will."

3 I also saw before the throne another great multitude whom no one could count, from every nation and tribe and people and ongue, which was constantly increasing by reason of the angels' carrying up the souls of God's saints, who had died in the world, so that the sound grew louder, and they cried: "Amen! Blessing and glory and wisdom and thanksgiving and honor and power and might be to our God for ever. Amen!"

4 In short, I saw lightning,brilliance, effulgence, and ineffable glory, and heard sounds and noise overpowering, all more joyful and wonderful than our eyes, ears, or hearts can comprehend.

5 Terrified by the vision of these glorious heavenly things, I fell before the majestic throne, ashamed of my sinfulness, of being a man of unclean lips, and cried: "The Lord, the Lord, the Lord God mighty, merciful, and gracious, slow to anger and plenteous in mercy and in truth; His mercy is upon thousands, and He forgives our iniquities, trangressions, and sins!" Lord, have mercy upon me, a sinner, for the sake of Jesus Christ!

CHAPTER LIII

THE PILGRIM IS RECEIVED AMONG GOD'S OWN

When I concluded, my Savior, Jesus Christ, addressed me from the midst of that throne in these delectable words: "Do not fear, my beloved, for I, your Redeemer, am with you; I am your comforter, be not afraid. Behold, your iniquity is taken away and your sin is blotted out. Rejoice and be glad, for your name is written among these, and if you will serve me faithfully, you shall become one of them. Whatever you have seen, use it in the fear of me, and in time you shall behold greater things than these. Guard yourself in the calling with which I have called you and walk in the way to glory that I have pointed out to you. As long as I leave you in the world, remain there as a pilgrim, a stranger, an alien, and a guest; but with me you are a member of my household, for I grant you the right of citizenship. Therefore, seek to have your conversation here, and have your mind ever lifted up to me as constantly as you can, but condescend to your neighbors as low as possible. Make use of the earthly things as long as you live on earth, but determined against the world and the flesh. Guard within yourself the wisdom I gave you, but outwardly observe the simplicity I commanded you. Have a vocal heart, but a silent tongue. Be sensitive to the sufferings of your neighbors, but inured to the wrongs inflicted upon yourself. Serve me alone with your soul, but with your body whomsoever you can or must. What I command, do, what I lay upon you, bear. Be restrained toward the world, but intimate with me. Remain in the world with your body, but with me with your heart. If you do these things, blessed are you, and it shall be well with you. Depart now, my beloved, and persevere in your calling to the end, joyfully using the solace which I have brought you."

CHAPTER LIV

THE CONCLUSION OF IT ALL

Suddenly the vision vanished from my eyes and I, falling on my knees and lifting my eyes to heaven, thanked my Redeemer as well as I could in these words:

"Blessed art Thou, O Lord my God, and worthy of eternal praise and exaltation, and blessed is the name of Thy glory, revered and all-glorious to all ages. Let Thine angels glorify Thee, and all Thy saints proclaim Thy praises. For Thou art great in power, and Thy wisdom is unsearchable; Thy mercy is above all Thy works. I will glorify Thee, O Lord, as long as I live, and will sing of Thy holy name as long as I exist; for Thou hast given me joy by Thy mercy, and hast filled my mouth with raptures; Thou hast snatched me out of violent torrents, and hast plucked me out of deep whirlpools, and hast placed my feet in safety. I have strayed far from Thee, my God, eternal sweetness, but Thou in Thy pity hast come nigh unto me. I went astray, but Thou hast recalled me. I have wandered about, not knowing where to g, but Thou has led me to the right path. I have gone astray , and have lost Thee as well as myself, but Thou hast overtaken me and hast returned me to myself as well as to Thee. I approached the very bitterness of hell, but Thou hast overtaken me and hast returned me to myself as well as to Thee. I approached the very bitterness of hell, but Thou hast pulled me back and hast brought me to the very sweetness of heaven. Therefore, bless the Lord, O my soul, and all that is within me bless His holy name. My heart is fixed, O God, my heart is fixed: I will sing and give praise to Thee. For Thou art higher than all height and deeper than all depth,wonderful, glorius, and full of mercy. Woe to the senseless souls which leave Thee, imagining to find peace elsewhere; for aside from Thee neither heaven, nor earth, nor the abyss possesses it; for in Thee alone is everlasting rest. Heaven and earth were made by Thee, and are good and beautiful and desirable because Thou hast made them; but they are neither as good nor as desirable as Thou, their Creator; therefore, they cannot satisfy nor suffice for souls seeking happiness. Thou art, O Lord, the fulness of all plentitude, and our hearts are restless until they find rest in Thee. Late have I come to love Thee, Thou beauty eternal, for late have I come to know Thee. But I came to know Thee when Thou, O heavenly brightness, hast shined upon me. Let him refrain from praising Thee who has not known Thy loving kindness: but all that is within me confess the Lord. Oh, who shall grant me that my heart may be charmed with Thee, O eternal Fragrance, so that I may forget all that is not Thyself, my God! Do not hide Thyself from my heart, O beauty most beautiful. If external things obscure Thee, may no longer lose Thee. Restrain me, Lord, lead me, bear me, that I no longer stray from Thee and fall. Grant that I may love Thee with an eternal love, and beside Thee love no thing, except for Thy sake and in Thee, O endles love! But what else shall I say, my Lord? Here I am,Thine I am; I am Thine own, Thine eternally. I renounce heaven and earth that I may have Thee alone. Only do not deny me Thyself and I have enough, to all eternity, unchangeably, I have enough in Thee alone. My soul and my body exult in Thee, Thou living God; Oh, when shall I go and appear before Thy face? Whenever it be Thy will, my Lord and God, take me, for here I am, I stand ready; call me whenever Thou desirest,whichever way Thou desirest, and however Thou desirest. I will go whithersoever Thou commandest and will perform whatsoever Thou commandest. May Thy good Spirit guide me and lead me among the snares of the world as in a plain, and may Thy lovingkIndness accompany me in my journeys. Lead me through this sorrowful darkness of the world to the light eternal. Amen and Amen."

GLORIA IN EXCELSIS DEO

ET IN TERRA PAX
HOMINIBUS BONAE VOLUNTATIS*

*Glory to God in the highest, and on earth peace to men of goodwill.

  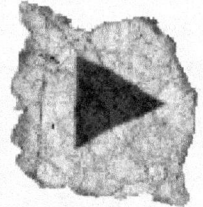